BUSHWHACKED!

Something whistled past his ear and the grulla went down, hard.

Instinct took over as the horse fell. Boyd kicked his feet free from the stirrups and threw himself out of the saddle. He landed awkwardly, his shoulder striking painfully against the hard-packed dirt of the road, but that was better than having a dead horse land on his leg and pin him down.

Another bullet slammed into the ground not far from Boyd's head, throwing dust into his eyes. He scrambled to his feet and flung himself forward, vaulting over the grulla's body to land on the far side of the horse, away from the bushwhacker—or bush-whackers, since he wasn't sure just how many of the sons of bitches were shooting at him.

Boyd waited until another shot had smacked into the grulla's body, then lifted himself and reached quickly for the stock of the rifle. His fingers closed around it, and he yanked it from the saddle boot. A bullet whined past his head. Boyd took another deep breath, then raised up and thrust the barrel of the rifle over the body of the horse. The wooded ridge came into his sights and he squeezed the trigger. The .70-caliber kicked hard against his shoulder as the rifle blasted. He ducked behind the grulla again.

There! At least the bastard would know now that he still had some fangs.

Boyd's breath hissed between his teeth as the bush-whacker fired three times, fast. . . .

McMASTERS

SILVER CREEK
SHOWDOWN

LEE MORGAN

JOVE BOOKS, NEW YORK

SILVER CREEK SHOWDOWN

A Jove Book / published by arrangement with
the author

PRINTING HISTORY
Jove edition / August 1995

ISBN: 0-515-11682-3

A JOVE BOOK®
Jove Books are published by The Berkley Publishing Group,
200 Madison Avenue, New York, New York 10016.
JOVE and the "J" design are trademarks
belonging to Jove Publications, Inc.

PRINTED IN THE UNITED STATES OF AMERICA

10 9 8 7 6 5 4 3 2 1

One

The settlement of Silver Creek looked just like a hundred other cow towns Boyd McMasters had seen in the West—right down to the man who came flying backwards through the batwing doors of a saloon to land with a puff of dust in the street in front of Boyd's horse.

The grulla shied nervously away from the man, but Boyd brought the horse under control with an expert hand. A second later there was a huge crash of glass as another man came sailing through the saloon's big front window. Boyd heard men yelling and women screaming, the thud of fists against flesh and bone, and the sharp splintering of wood as tables and chairs were overturned and shattered into kindling.

There was trouble in Silver Creek, all right, Boyd thought. This fight might not have anything to do with the problems that had brought him here, but it was going to wreak some havoc anyway.

And there was always the chance that it *might* be involved in the job too.

So far he hadn't heard any guns going off, which was good. As long as the men inside the saloon were just brawling with their fists, there was a better than even chance nobody would be killed. It was when the guns came out that men died.

Boyd heeled the grulla forward, reining the horse toward

the hitch rail in front of the hardware store next to the saloon. He swung down from the saddle, looped the reins around the rail and jerked them tight, then strode back down the street to where the first man who had been knocked out of the saloon had pushed himself onto hands and knees. The man knelt there, shaking his head slowly. Beads of blood welled from a cut on his cheek and rolled down his face to drip off his chin, going first one way, then the other as he shook his head.

Boyd reached down and grasped the man's arm. "Let me give you a hand, mister," he said as he hauled the man to his feet. There was more strength in Boyd's rangy frame than most people would have thought from looking at him. "What's going on in there?"

The man's lips were swollen from a punch and his voice was thick as he replied, "We're tryin' to teach those bastards from the Rocking T a lesson they won't forget any time soon!"

It was just what Boyd had figured. The battle was between cowhands from a couple of rival ranches. He said, "Who do you ride for, amigo?"

The man backhanded some of the blood from his face. "The JF Connected, of course. Thanks for your help, mister, but lemme go. I gotta get back in there and help my pards!"

With that, he pulled away from Boyd's grasp and launched into a stumbling run that carried him to the entrance of the saloon. He slapped the batwings aside and plunged back into the melee.

Boyd glanced at the other victim of the fight, the one who had come crashing through the window of the saloon. The man was still lying on the ground with broken glass scattered all around him. He wasn't moving, but Boyd could tell he was still breathing. Boyd walked over to the man, the shards of glass crunching under his boots, and hooked a toe under the man's shoulder to roll him over onto his back. Boyd hunkered beside him and slapped his face lightly a couple of times, backhand and forehand. The man's eyelids started to flutter.

"Who do you ride for?" Boyd asked when the man's eyes finally opened.

"Hunh . . . what the hell . . ."

"Who do you ride for?" Boyd repeated.

"R-Rockin' T . . ."

Boyd stood up and let the man lapse back into semi-consciousness. There was a faint smile on Boyd's lips as he turned and strode toward the entrance of the saloon.

He wondered fleetingly where the local law was. There was so much noise coming from the saloon that somebody packing a badge should have showed up by now. Even if the marshal didn't hear the ruckus, someone should have fetched him. A good two dozen citizens, maybe more, stood around in the street near the saloon, craning their necks to get a glimpse of the chaos inside through the busted-out window. Surely one of the townies had run down to the marshal's office by now to let him know what was going on.

Several men stood aside as Boyd walked up to the entrance. That wasn't surprising since he carried himself with an air of authority that came naturally to him, having once been a lawman himself. And he looked tough enough to back up just about anything he wanted to do too. He was a medium-sized, sandy-haired man, not an overpowering specimen physically, but his toughness was in his eyes and the tanned, weathered features of his face. He wore a fairly new light brown Stetson, a hickory-colored work shirt with the sleeves rolled up a couple of turns against the Texas heat, denim pants, and well-broken-in boots. Holstered on his right hip was a revolver he had modified himself with his gunsmithing skills, a .40-caliber on a sturdy .42 frame. He had the look of a man who could use a gun as well as work on one.

He pushed through the batwings after a second's pause to make sure no one would crash into him as soon as he stepped inside the saloon. The fracas was still going on, but it seemed to be concentrated on the far side of the room now. The saloon was one of the biggest buildings in Silver Creek, since it had two stories instead of just one, and the girls who worked here in spangled dresses and tights had retreated up the stairs to the balcony, where they now stood shouting encouragement down to the battlers below. Boyd saw a couple of bartenders venturing an occasional glance from down behind the hardwood bar that ran along the right-hand wall. To the left was a piano, and the fellow who normally played it, a gent with pomaded hair and sleeve garters, had turned over his bench and retreated behind it. A few men were sprawled senseless amidst the wreckage of several tables.

Boyd spotted the man he had helped up in the street outside. The JF Connected cowboy was now clubbing another man on top of the head with a mallet-like fist. The Rocking T puncher went down, but before the man from the JF Connected could find another adversary, somebody brought a chair crashing down on his head from behind. Boyd winced.

Somebody plucked at Boyd's sleeve, and he looked around to see a pasty-faced man in a cutaway coat. The man had a goatee and a thin mustache and was a gambler from the look of him. He said, "I'd steer clear of that donnybrook over there if I was you, my friend."

"How do you know I intend to take a hand?" Boyd asked.

"You have the look of a man who searches for trouble, assuming it doesn't find you first."

Boyd smiled a little, but the expression didn't reach his eyes. The gambler had him pegged, all right. Trouble had found him plenty of times in the past, and now his job was to look for it. Usually, it wasn't very hard to find.

Inclining his head toward the battling men, Boyd asked the gambler, "What started this?"

The nattily dressed man shrugged. "*Quién sabe?* They

don't really need a reason other than the fact that some of them ride for Jonas Fletcher and the others for Mike Torrance. That's plenty of motivation.''

Boyd nodded, and turned his attention back to the fracas in time to see one of the men reaching for a holstered gun.

The saloon was big, but not that big. If guns started going off, there was a good chance that innocent people would be struck by at least some of the flying bullets. Boyd's hand shot out and closed around the neck of a whiskey bottle that stood on a table within arm's reach of him. The waddy trying to fumble his gun from its holster was only about fifteen feet away from him. Boyd's arm flashed back and then forward, and the half-full bottle thumped heavily against the back of the cowboy's head. He forgot all about pulling his gun as he stumbled forward a couple of steps, went to his knees, then pitched onto his face, out cold.

''Good throw,'' the gambler said dryly over the shouts and screams. ''I'm Anthony Hagen.''

''Boyd McMasters.''

''When that fellow wakes up, he's not going to feel very friendly toward you, Mr. McMasters.''

Boyd's casual shrug told eloquently just how concerned he was about that possibility.

One of the struggling men suddenly broke free of the brawl and lunged toward the stairs that led to the balcony and the second floor. He had made it up only three of the steps when another man caught him from behind and jerked him around. The first man's hat had been knocked off, revealing thick, curly brown hair. His face was lean, his mouth wide and expressive. As he opened his mouth to yell his dismay, Boyd saw that there was a wide gap between his front teeth. The man who had caught him had broad, massive shoulders, and he seemed to have no trouble picking up the first man by an arm and a leg and slinging him back into the middle of the pile. Several men went down under the onslaught, sprawling every which way.

The curly-haired man who had served as a makeshift

battering ram landed heavily and rolled over several times, then came up on his hands and knees and struggled to his feet. This time, instead of trying to escape up the stairs, he made a break for the entrance. Boyd had to step aside hurriedly to avoid being run down. The fleeing man knocked the batwings back and ran into the street.

The gambler, Hagen, laughed. "Chuck doesn't have much stomach for fighting," he commented.

"Chuck?" Boyd asked.

"Chuck Fletcher. Jonas's little brother."

Boyd nodded, and since Hagen seemed willing to answer questions, asked another. "How come the marshal hasn't put in an appearance yet?"

"He'll show up as soon as he realizes what's going on."

"You mean nobody's gone to fetch him by now?"

Hagen gave him a look that indicated disbelief. "What, and interfere with a fight between the Rocking T and the JF Connected? This town depends on those two spreads for its livelihood, Mr. McMasters. Nobody wants to risk offending either Jonas Fletcher or Mike Torrance. Their men do pretty much as they please in Silver Creek."

"So instead of running for the law, the owner of this place lets those boys wreck it? That's hard to believe."

"Believe it," Hagen said. "I own this saloon. And I know that Jonas and Mike will stand good for any damages."

Boyd nodded slowly. If that was the way Hagen wanted to do business, that was his affair.

At that moment, the batwings were slapped open again and a lanky, middle-aged man with graying hair and a sweeping mustache hurried in with a shotgun in his hands. There was a tin star pinned to his shirt. He bellowed, "What in blazes—"

"Please, Marshal!" Hagen said. "Don't fire that scatter-gun into the ceiling again. We like to never got the holes patched from last time."

The star-packer blinked and said, "Yeah, but—"

That was as far as he got before Boyd saw one of the combatants turn toward the door with a gun in his hand.

Boyd palmed out his own revolver, not with the blindingly fast speed of a shootist but rather with the quick, sure efficiency of a man long accustomed to handling guns. The cowboy was lifting his pistol and almost had it lined up on the marshal when Boyd's gun roared.

There hadn't been time for any fancy shooting. A shot directed toward the man's head or torso could have gone past him and hit somebody else if Boyd had missed. So he shot toward the man's feet instead, intending the bullet as a distraction more than anything else, even though it went against the grain for him to pull trigger without having someone's death as his goal. If he missed, the slug likely wouldn't hit anything except the planks of the floor.

He didn't miss. The gun-wielding cowboy let out a howl of pain and jumped several inches in the air. He went over backwards, landing on his rump, and the impact was so jarring that he dropped his Colt. It thudded to the floor beside him, unfired. He had come down with his right leg stretched out in front of him, and he stared disbelievingly at the smoking hole in the toe of his boot. Then he swayed and his body fell backwards. His head thumped against the floor.

A shocked silence had fallen over the saloon after the explosion of the gunshot. Everybody stared at Boyd, including the marshal and Anthony Hagen. Boyd replaced the round he had fired with a cartridge from one of the loops on his belt, then slid the gun back into leather. He nodded toward the man he had shot and said, "Somebody better pull that fella's boot off and take a look at his foot. I might've blown a toe off."

"Who the hell are you?" demanded the marshal.

"Name's Boyd McMasters."

"What'd you shoot that fella for?"

Boyd frowned a little in surprise. "Looked to me like he

was about to shoot you, Marshal. I didn't figure you'd like that.''

"Mike Torrance ain't goin' to like it neither when he finds out you've maybe crippled one of his best hands!'' The lawman gestured curtly at the injured man. "Somebody yank his boot off!''

One of the men who had been fighting only a few moments earlier leaned over and pulled the man's boot off. The sock underneath was bloody. The man who had taken the boot off looked up and reported solemnly, "Looks like his middle toe's plumb gone.''

"Shit!'' the marshal said, his displeasure obviously heartfelt. He turned to Boyd. "You're a stranger here, mister. What the hell brings you to Silver Creek, anyway?''

"My job,'' Boyd replied grimly. "And right about now, I'm beginning to wish I'd never heard of this sorry little place!''

Two

"Right there," Warren McMasters had said a few days earlier as he poked a blunt fingertip at a spot on the map tacked to the wall of his office in Oklahoma City. "About a day's ride northwest of Fort Worth. You can ride the train down there or take the stagecoach, whichever you'd like."

"I'll pick a good horse and ride him," Boyd told his brother. His expression and tone of voice were both sour as he went on. "I've been around people too damned much lately. I need some time to myself."

Warren sighed and sat down behind his desk. Boyd was slouched in a straight-backed chair in front of the desk, his hat on the floor beside the chair. He looked a lot better now than he had a few months earlier, when he had showed up in Warren's office after a long binge of grief, self-pity, hard drinking, and generally self-destructive behavior, but he still could have easily been mistaken for a no-account drifter . . . if not for the fact that his boots and his gun were so well cared for.

"I'm not sure it's a good idea for you to be alone too much," Warren said as he plucked a sheet of paper from the welter of documents atop his desk. As the head of the Cattleman's Protective Association, the enforcement arm of the larger Cattleman's Association, he spent most of his time doing paperwork. The agents out in the field—men like his brother Boyd—were the ones who took action.

Boyd took out a clasp knife, unfolded it, and used it to cut the tip off a Primero cigarillo he slid from his shirt pocket. When he had the cigarillo shaped to suit him, he lit it with a kitchen match he struck on the sole of his boot. If he had any extra smokes, he didn't offer one to his brother. He held the Primero between his teeth and said around it, "You know it's been a damned long time since I was drunk, Warren. What's the matter, you afraid that if I'm by myself too much I'll wind up *borracho* again?"

"It could happen," Warren said curtly. He didn't need to mention the reason Boyd had wound up a pathetic drunk in the first place. The memories of Boyd's late wife Hannah were always with him, floating around like a particularly stubborn ghost. Boyd had tried to banish them with whiskey, but that hadn't worked, of course. Now he was learning to live with the hurt. It never went away completely, but at least on some days it wasn't quite as sharp as it had once been.

Boyd puffed on the Primero, blew gray smoke to the side, and said, "You've got my word I won't mess up the job by drinking too much on the way down to Texas, Warren. If that's not good enough for you . . . well, screw you and the horse you *didn't* ride in on."

Warren flushed and said, "Your word's good enough for me, Boyd. Always has been."

"So what's the job?"

Warren consulted the piece of paper in his hand. "One of the Association's members, a rancher named Jonas Fletcher, has lost some stock. He wants us to investigate."

"How much stock?"

Warren shook his head and said, "Fletcher's letter didn't specify any particular number. He just said the loss had damaged him very much and he needed us to try to recover the stolen animals if possible."

"What about the local law?"

"There's a marshal in the town of Silver Creek and a

county sheriff, of course, but I gather that neither of them have been very effective.''

"Fletcher could ask the Rangers for help," Boyd suggested.

"It's true there's a Ranger post not far away, at a place called Veal Station, but evidently they don't regard the case as, ah, pressing enough to assign any men to it.''

Boyd sat up straighter. "Hell, Warren," he said, "this is just some penny-ante rustling that's so small the locals can't be bothered with it. So this Fletcher writes a letter to the CPA and asks for a field agent to be sent all the way down there. It's a damned waste of time if you ask me.''

"Nobody did," Warren reminded him, a steely edge to his voice. "Jonas Fletcher is a member in good standing of the Association, and as such is entitled to our investigative and enforcement services if he deems them necessary. You're the only man I have available right now. I'd send Captain Reese and those two friends of his if they weren't already off on another job up in Colorado. Now, will you accept this assignment or not?''

For a long moment, Boyd didn't answer. Finally, though, he sighed and said, "Sometimes you ask a hell of a lot for a hundred bucks a month wages and five dollars a day expense money, Warren.''

His brother leaned back in his chair, trying not to smile in satisfaction. "You ought to be able to clear this up without much trouble, Boyd. It'll almost be a vacation for you.''

"I don't take vacations," Boyd said coldly. "I stopped caring about such things a while back.''

"I know." Warren's voice was soft, and he didn't meet his brother's eyes. "I appreciate this.''

Boyd picked up his hat, stood, and leaned over to put out the stub of his cigarillo in the ashtray on Warren's desk. Then he turned and walked out of the office. He had places to go and things to do before he left Oklahoma City and headed for North Texas.

• • •

Martha Blair threw her head back so that her thick brown hair swirled around her shoulders. She put her hands on Boyd's chest to balance herself as her hips pumped back and forth furiously. Her back was slightly arched, which thrust her breasts forward. Boyd reached up with both hands and cupped them, letting his thumbs rub teasingly around the hard, pebbled brown nipples that crowned each soft mound of flesh. Martha groaned, caught her lower lip between her teeth, closed her eyes, and pumped that much harder. Boyd didn't have to do much, just lift his hips a little now and then to meet her thrusts. His manhood was already buried in her just about as deeply as it would go.

The room in the neat, whitewashed frame house on the outskirts of Oklahoma City was dim, the curtains drawn over the windows. Late afternoon sunlight peeked through a few gaps, however, slanting brightly to the rug on the floor beside the bed. There was enough light in the room for Boyd to see the flush that crept over Martha's face and shoulders, the beads of sweat that sprang out on her forehead. He was pretty warm himself, but it was a good heat.

A cleansing heat.

When he was with Martha, the memories of Hannah receded more than ever, and not just when they were in bed together either. He could be sitting in her parlor and talking to her, or just straddling a chair in her kitchen and watching her shell peas or do some such chore, and realize suddenly that the hurt had almost gone away. Of course, that realization always made fresh waves of guilt flood in on him, as if he was somehow being disloyal to Hannah by no longer wallowing in misery over her death. No matter how many times Warren told him that Hannah would have wanted him to get on with his life and put the past behind him, it was impossible for Boyd to do that completely.

But Martha had helped him, was still helping him. She dulled the pain better than whiskey ever had. His hands tightened on her breasts, holding on as if she might bounce right off him if he didn't. They helped each other, and today, after he had told her he was leaving again on another job for the Association, she seemed to need him even more than usual. Sometimes their lovemaking was soft and gentle, and other times were like this one, frenzied and urgent and filled with need. Boyd felt his climax approaching and tried to hold it off as long as possible. He didn't want Martha to feel let down.

She pushed herself higher until she was sitting up straight on him, his shaft probing her to the deepest point yet. Her breath rasped harshly in her throat. He raised his hands and she caught them, her fingers entwining with his. There was no holding off anymore. His hips surged up and he began to empty himself in her.

Martha cried out as he flooded her. She trembled, and her fingers tightened on his. At that moment, linked so strongly, they might as well have been one being instead of two. Almost. Something inside Boyd had never let him take that final step with his mind, no matter what he did with his body.

Martha drew in a great, gasping breath and collapsed on his chest. Her arms went around his neck, and he put his arms around her middle and returned the hug she gave him. He felt himself slip out of her, and she made a little noise of disappointment. Boyd slid one hand down to her rump and caressed the gently sloping hillocks of warm flesh. Martha's breath was hot on his skin as she buried her face against his shoulder.

After several long moments, she pushed herself up so that she could look at his face. She said, "Boyd, I . . ."

He laid a finger on her lips. Whatever she had been about to say, he didn't want to hear it. Both of them had great tragedies in their pasts, and it was fine for them to draw whatever help and comfort from each other that they could. But that was as far as it was likely to go, and they both knew it.

"I could use a drink," he said.

He saw something in Martha's eyes, a faint flicker of

pain. If he had wounded her, he was sorry, damned sorry. But there were things in him that were wounded too, things that were taking their own sweet time about healing—and maybe they never would. Until that time came, if it ever did, they both had to be reasonable. They had to be practical.

Even if it hurt.

She managed to smile, and her fingertips stroked his face for a second. Then she rolled off him and sat up on the edge of the bed. He watched her as she stood up, admiring the clean lines of her back and hips and legs until she covered them by wrapping a robe around herself. Over her shoulder, she said, "I think I could use a drink too," then left the room.

Boyd didn't know if she was coming back or if he was supposed to follow her. He got up, found his pants, and pulled them on. He put his shirt on but didn't button it, then walked barefoot from the bedroom into the kitchen. Martha had gotten a couple of glasses and a bottle from a cabinet. She had set the glasses on the table, and uncorked the bottle, and was pouring drinks for both of them. She handed one of the glasses to Boyd.

"Here's to the job," she said. "Good luck."

Boyd couldn't tell if there was bitterness in her voice or if she was being sincere.

He lifted the glass to his mouth, tossing back the whiskey. It burned going down. If he had ever been able to tell good whiskey from bad, the months-long binge had destroyed that ability in him. Now he drank whatever came his way and cared only about the fire that it kindled in his belly. He wasn't a drunk anymore; he could truly take the stuff or leave it, and unlike some, one sip of booze wasn't enough to start him on a bender again. But at moments like this, he was damned grateful for the kick the whiskey had. Somehow it made him see the world a little more clearly.

"I don't reckon I'll be gone long," he said. "Two weeks maybe. No more than three. It'd be less than that if I took the train down there. But I feel like riding."

"The fresh air will do you good," Martha said.

Now this time there was a definite edge of sarcasm in her voice, Boyd thought.

She sat down at the table, then sipped her drink and went on. "This assignment is about some rustling, you said?"

He nodded as he straddled one of the other chairs. "I'm not really sure what's going on down there. Warren didn't have a lot of information. Evidently some rancher who's a member of the Association has his back fur in an uproar over something, and Warren feels like it's my job to go down there and straighten things out. So I suppose that's what I'll do."

"What was the place called? Silver Creek?"

"That's right."

"Pretty name," Martha said. "Have you ever been there?"

"Not that I recall."

"Well, I'm sure you won't have any trouble straightening things out, as you put it. You're good at seeing what needs to be done about other people's problems."

Boyd's lips pressed together tightly. He wasn't sure how she could go from screwing him damn near senseless to making these sharp little comments in such a short period of time. But that was a woman for you, he guessed. If the Good Lord had intended for them to make sense, He wouldn't have given them tits and a pussy.

Of course, right about now she was probably thinking the same thing about him and every other creature on God's green earth who had a cock and a pair of balls. . . .

She broke into his thoughts by saying, "Boyd . . . I really don't mind you going. I know it's your job, and I'm very glad you found something that you can do."

He shrugged his shoulders. "Can't go back to being a lawman. This is something I know how to do."

"And you are good at it. I mean that."

"I know."

She reached across the table and caught his hand. "You go on down there to Silver Creek and do whatever needs to be done. And when you're finished, come back here to me."

"I always intended to, Martha," he told her. "I always intended to."

Three

Marshal John Durkee pointed to the ladderback chair in front of his desk. "Sit down," he told Boyd. "I want to hear about this."

Boyd lowered himself onto the chair and cuffed back his hat. He said, "You know, Marshal, some folks might think it strange that you don't arrest the fella who tried to throw down on you, or the men who caused a couple of hundred dollars worth of damage in that saloon. But the man who maybe saved your life and helped break up that fight, him you haul off to the hoosegow."

The lawman sat down and glared across the desk. "You see any cuffs on your wrists?" he demanded. "You see any iron bars in front of your face? I told you, McMasters, you ain't under arrest. I just figured it'd be a good idea to get you out of Hagen's place 'fore any more shootin' broke out. And I want to hear about this so-called job of yours too."

They had left the saloon after Hagen had assured them that the trouble was over, at least for the time being. With all the friction between the Rocking T and the JF Connected, it was only a matter of time until another ruckus broke out. But Boyd had a strong suspicion that the hostility between the two spreads was tied in with the assignment that had brought him here to Silver Creek.

He reached for a cigarillo and asked, "Mind if I smoke?"

"I sure do," Durkee said with a curt nod. "I got nothin' against tobacco, but I want you concentratin' on tellin' me just what you're doin' in my town."

Boyd left the Primero in his pocket and leaned back in the chair. The marshal was an easy man to dislike, and Boyd told himself to hold on to his temper. Otherwise he would likely make an enemy right at the start of a man who could possibly make his job easier . . . or a lot harder, if Durkee took it in his mind to do that.

"All right," Boyd said. He reached inside his shirt and took out an oilskin pouch. He usually carried the pouch in his saddlebags, but he had removed it earlier, before riding into Silver Creek, and put it where it would be handier. Now he tossed it onto Durkee's desk and went on. "My credentials are in there."

"Got yourself some bona fides, eh?" Durkee picked up the pouch, opened it, and took out several folded sheets of paper. He spread them out on his desk and took his time reading them, his lips moving just a little as he did so. When he was finished, he looked up at Boyd. "Says here you're a field agent from the Cattleman's Protective Association with the rank of captain."

"That's what it says," Boyd agreed.

Durkee replaced the documents in the pouch and passed it back to Boyd. "Bein' a captain in a civilian organization don't mean a whole lot. It ain't like you're a real lawman."

"Most places, the authorities are happy to cooperate with us. In some parts of the West, CPA agents are about all the law there is."

"Well, that ain't the case around here," Durkee said indignantly. "We got law in Silver Creek, mister. You're lookin' at it."

Boyd nodded. "I never said otherwise," he pointed out, keeping his tone conciliatory even though it cost him quite an effort. He was getting damned tired of this old mossback and his cheap tin badge. "In fact, I expect we can help each other."

The marshal looked dubious. "How d'you figure that?"

"You've got trouble in your town because of the way the crews of the JF Connected and the Rocking T go at each other. I'd be willing to bet that fight today wasn't the first one between those two bunches."

Durkee snorted. "Not by a damn sight. Ain't a week goes by there's not a brawl like that one. The townspeople are gettin' pure-dee fed up with it. But what can I do? Even if I could throw the whole lot of 'em in jail—which I can't, seein' as how I only got two deputies and neither one of them is really worth a plug—Fletcher and Torrance would just come into town and pay the fines for their boys and raise hell with me for arrestin' 'em in the first place! How the hell's a lawman supposed to keep the peace in a situation like that?"

Boyd held up his hands, palms out, and said, "Calm down, Marshal. I don't blame you for being upset. I'm here to put a stop to the rustling that's got everybody around here in an uproar. Maybe when that's done, Fletcher's outfit and Torrance's boys can get along."

"Rustlin'?" Durkee asked with a frown. "What rustlin'?"

"Isn't that what's got everybody upset?" Boyd was frowning too, and hoping that Warren hadn't gotten the assignments mixed up somehow.

"Well, I guess you could call it rustlin'," Durkee said slowly, "though I never thought of it like that. Jonas Fletcher *did* lose some stock."

"How much?"

"Four head."

For a second, Boyd thought his ears were playing tricks on him. He couldn't have heard the marshal's answer correctly. "Four head?" he repeated. "Don't you mean four hundred? Or at least forty?"

Durkee shook his head. "Nope. Four was what I said,

and four's what I meant. I may be gettin' a mite long in the tooth, but I ain't addle-brained.''

It was all Boyd could do to rein in his temper. From what Warren had told him in Oklahoma City, he figured the rustling going on around Silver Creek to be pretty small potatoes . . . but *four* head of stolen stock? Warren had sent him all the way down here for *four* head?

Boyd stood up, took a deep breath, and reached for his wallet. How much could four cattle be worth, a couple of hundred bucks at the most? He said angrily, "I'll pay for the damn brutes and charge it off to the Association, and then maybe Fletcher'll be happy again. How much were they worth?''

"Well, I ain't exactly sure . . . you'd have to ask Fletcher about that . . . but I hear tell it's twenty thousand dollars.''

The whiskey must have damaged his brain more than he had thought, Boyd told himself. He could have sworn that the marshal had just said those stolen cattle were worth twenty thousand dollars. He swallowed hard, hoping he wasn't losing his mind, and said, "Twenty thousand dollars for four cows?''

Durkee shook his head. "Not cows. Bulls. Four of 'em. Fletcher was askin' five thousand apiece for 'em, or so I heard, and he got his price. The buyers are supposed to be comin' in any time now to pick 'em up.''

Boyd sat down again. This was starting to make a little more sense. Maybe he wasn't crazy after all. "These are prize bulls you're talking about?''

"That's right. Yearlings. Jonas Fletcher brought their daddy over from England a couple of years ago. Biggest, ugliest brute you ever did see. Fletcher paid eight thousand for him, and he figures to make that up and more from this first crop of bulls. Goin' to revolutionize the cattle-breedin' industry in this part of the country, or so he says. Folks don't care for longhorns that much anymore. Too tough and stringy—sort of like old coots like me.'' Durkee laughed.

Boyd leaned back again and cocked his booted right foot

on his left knee. He was beginning to understand a lot more now. He said, "I reckon Fletcher blames this fella Mike Torrance for stealing those bulls."

Durkee nodded. "Him and Torrance don't get along to start with, on account of Belinda and Griff."

"You lost me again," Boyd said. "Who are Belinda and Griff?"

"Well, you see, Fletcher and Torrance are both widowers. Both of 'em got one youngster—a boy and a girl."

"Let me guess," Boyd said. "Fletcher has a daughter named Belinda and Torrance a son named Griff."

"Got that one right on the nail, McMasters. And those two young'uns—"

"Think they're in love with each other," Boyd finished for him.

Durkee looked surprised. "How'd you know that?"

"It's my business to figure things out, remember? Some folks call us field agents range detectives."

"Well, you're right about Belinda and Griff. They'd up and get married if their daddies'd let 'em. And to tell you the truth, I reckon Mike Torrance don't think it's such a bad idea. He never was as touchy about things as Jonas Fletcher."

"Then it's Fletcher who won't hear of a marriage."

"He don't even want them two kids seein' each other," Durkee said. "And that's why he figures Mike Torrance— and maybe Griff along with him—stole those bulls. He thinks they're tryin' to get back at him because he don't want his daughter havin' anything to do with Torrance's boy."

Boyd sat up straight again and put his hands on his knees. He wanted a smoke, and he wanted a drink, and he couldn't decide which one he wanted more. He had expected a nice, clear-cut case when he started down here. Track down a few rustlers, kill the sons of bitches if he had to or turn them over to the law if he didn't, and then go back to Oklahoma City.

Instead, he found his plate filled with some missing prize bulls, a couple of feuding cattle barons, and a damned romance that was like something out of that old Englishman's plays, the ones that the traveling acting troupes put on all the time. He wasn't going to be able to straighten this out with guns and fists, at least not totally.

Durkee sat back, folded his hands over his little potbelly, and grinned across the desk at Boyd. "There you go," he said. "That's the story of what's goin' on around here. What do you figure to do about it, Mr. Cattleman's Protective Association?"

Boyd could think of a good start that involved putting his fist in the middle of the old lawman's shit-eating grin. But that wouldn't accomplish a damned thing except to make him feel better for the moment. Instead, he stood up and said, "I'm going to get something to eat, then I'll ride out to the JF Connected and pay a call on Fletcher. After all, he's the reason I'm here in this friendly little settlement of yours, Marshal." He didn't bother trying to keep the sarcasm out of his voice. "You think you can tell me where to find Fletcher's spread?"

"Sure. Take the road west out of town for about eight miles. You'll find a trail branchin' off to the north and one to the south. The one to the south leads to Fletcher's place."

"And the one going north?"

"That'll take you right to Torrance's Rocking T."

"Somehow I figured that's what you'd say," Boyd muttered. "Sounds to me like the main road runs right between the two spreads."

"That it does. Which means you'd best keep your eyes peeled. Those punchers like to take potshots at each other from time to time."

"I'll bear it in mind," Boyd said dryly.

"I'll even tell you a good place to eat," Durkee said. "Go right on down the street here to the Red Top Cafe. You can't miss it. Best food in town."

"Thanks." Boyd hesitated, then added, "I hope we can work together on this without getting in each other's way, Marshal."

"Oh, you won't be in my way, boy. I intend to let you handle it any way you like, long as you don't cause trouble for me here in town. Those missin' bulls, that's out of my jurisdiction."

Boyd couldn't bring himself to like the smug old lawman, but he appreciated the information. He said as much and left the marshal's office, heading down the street toward a squat building made of huge chunks of reddish sandstone mortared together. The place had a red tile roof, and in front of it was a rock porch with a wooden awning over it. A gaudy sign attached to the awning announced simply *The Red Top*.

The building had batwing doors like a saloon, but the smells that drifted out into the street from it were those of chicken-fried steak, cornbread, beans, and hot sauce instead of whiskey, smoke, sweat, and piss. Boyd paused in the doorway and breathed deeply, his stomach letting him know just how long it had been since he had eaten.

"Hey! Hey, mister, over here!"

Boyd looked in the direction of the eager voice that was calling him from inside, and saw the man who had done his best to escape the brawl in the saloon earlier. Chuck Fletcher, Boyd recalled. The saloonkeeper Hagen had told him Chuck was the brother of Jonas Fletcher.

Chuck had been bareheaded when Boyd saw him earlier, but now he was wearing a broad-brimmed, high-crowned black hat that was shoved back on his thatch of curly brown hair. He was also wearing high-topped boots, denim pants, and a black-and-white cowhide vest over a work shirt. The range garb looked vaguely ridiculous on him, Boyd thought. Chuck reminded him of dudes who came out from the East and believed that clothes made the cowboy. But if he was Jonas Fletcher's brother, he likely wasn't a dude at all. Boyd started toward the table where Chuck was sitting.

Maybe he could find out some more about the situation that was causing so much tension around here.

Chuck hopped to his feet when Boyd reached the table. "Sit down, sit down," the young man urged. "Why don't you join me? I was about to eat."

"Don't mind if I do," Boyd said as he sank into one of the empty chairs.

"I'm Chuck Fletcher."

"Boyd McMasters." Boyd took the hand Chuck thrust across the table at him and shook it.

"I know. I heard all about what happened at Hagen's place after I, ah, left. You shot the gun right out of Mitch Riley's hand."

"Well . . . not exactly. I shot him in the foot and he dropped his gun."

Chuck waved off that explanation. "I heard you're the fastest man on the draw who's ever come to Silver Creek."

Boyd frowned. The last thing he wanted was for somebody to start spreading rumors that he was some sort of gunfighter. He began, "I wouldn't say that—"

That was as far as he got before a man suddenly stepped up behind Chuck, put a gun to the back of his head, and said harshly, "I ought to blow your goddamned brains out."

Four

Boyd had seen the man walking behind Chuck's chair, but hadn't really paid any attention to him until the man suddenly pulled a gun. Now, as the stranger ground the barrel of the revolver into the back of Chuck's head, Boyd stiffened and started to come up out of his seat.

"Don't try it, mister!" the gunman ordered curtly. "I'll kill this bastard, I swear I will."

The gunman looked like a townie, not a killer, Boyd thought. The sort of man who would work at a freight company or a lumberyard. He didn't seem too comfortable holding the gun. But he was angry enough that he would use the weapon if he had to; Boyd could see that much in his eyes.

Chuck's eyes were wide with fear and he seemed to be frozen in his chair. After a moment, he was able to say, "My brother won't like it if you kill me, Clooney."

"I don't care what your brother likes or don't like," Clooney grated. "I want to know what the hell you thought you were doing with that pig."

"Pig?" Chuck asked innocently. "What pig?"

"The one you put in my parlor right before my wife's sewing circle had their weekly meeting there! Some of those ladies like to fainted when they saw a four-hundred-pound sow in the middle of the rug. And what that thing did to my wife's favorite sofa . . ."

Boyd relaxed a little. It seemed unlikely that anybody would kill a man over what sounded like some sort of practical joke. You never knew, though, especially when the man holding the gun was an amateur and not a professional. He kept a close eye on Clooney.

"I don't know what you're talking about," Chuck was saying. "You and I are friends, Clooney. I wouldn't embarrass you that way."

"You don't have any friends," Clooney said bitterly, "just victims. Well, I'm here to tell you that I'm not going to stand for it anymore, Chuck. You're going to pay me for the damage that porker did, and I don't want anything more to do with you."

"Clooney, I'm . . . I'm shocked that you don't believe me when I tell you—"

"I asked around the neighborhood," Clooney interrupted. "Andy Simmons saw you with a pig headed toward the back of my house. That's proof enough for me."

Not wanting to spook the gunman, Boyd kept both hands in plain sight on the table as he said, "I haven't known you for long, Chuck, but if it was me, I wouldn't want to get shot over a pig. You'd better 'fess up."

With an embarrassed grin on his face, Chuck said, "Well, yeah, it was me. I just thought it might liven up that ladies' sewing circle to have a pig there. I'm sorry, Clooney. I didn't mean any harm."

"You never mean any harm, you . . . you damned jackass! How a normal fella like Jonas Fletcher ended up with a brother like you is a plumb mystery to me, boy." Clooney sighed and took his gun from Chuck's head. As he holstered it, he went on. "I'll send Jonas a bill for the damages."

"And I'm sure he'll pay it," Chuck said solemnly.

"One of these days . . . one of these days . . ." Unable to find the words to finish his thought, Clooney stalked out of the cafe, shaking his head.

"There goes a touchy hombre," Chuck said quietly,

leaning forward and inclining his head toward the departing Clooney. "He acts like he never saw a pig in anybody's parlor before."

Boyd said, "I get the feeling your brother is used to paying for the trouble you get into."

"Hey, it's not like I don't earn my keep around the ranch," Chuck protested. "I may not look like it, but I'm a top hand."

"You're right—you don't look like it." Boyd glanced around for a waitress. The brief confrontation had almost made him forget how hungry he was . . . almost.

The place had fallen silent while Clooney was holding a gun to Chuck's head, but now that the danger was over, things were rapidly returning to normal. Every seat at the counter next to the door that connected to the kitchen was full, and most of the tables covered with checked table-cloths were occupied too. A pretty young woman in a ging-ham dress came over to the table where Boyd and Chuck sat and asked, "Are you gents ready to order?"

For an instant, Boyd felt a sharp pang in his chest. The woman was not only young and pretty, she was also blond and reminded him at first glance of Hannah. A longer look told him there wasn't really any resemblance at all, and he forced down the bitter memories that welled up in his mind.

"What's good today?" he made himself ask.

"Why, everything on the menu, of course," the blonde said, her face dimpling in a smile. "But I'd recommend either the beef stew or the chicken-fried steak."

"I'll take the steak," Boyd told her. "It's too hot for stew. Plenty of mashed potatoes and gravy on the side, some green beans if you've got 'em, and don't spare the biscuits."

"Some fresh-made lemonade with that?"

Boyd smiled and nodded.

"I'll have the same," Chuck said. "Got any peach cob-bler?"

"We sure do, Mr. Fletcher."

"I'll have that too then."

The waitress nodded and started to move away toward the kitchen, but then she hesitated and looked back. "Mr. Fletcher . . . nobody else is going to be pulling a gun on you in here, are they?"

"Not that I know of."

"Good," the young woman said fervently. "It's mighty hard getting bloodstains up off this floor."

"You'd think these people had never seen a gun before," Chuck muttered as the waitress disappeared into the kitchen.

"Things like that happen to you often?" Boyd asked.

"Of course not! Well, not too often. But you don't want to hear about my problems. What brings you to Silver Creek, Mr. McMasters?"

For a moment, Boyd didn't answer, turning over in his mind just how much he ought to confide in Chuck, who was obviously something of a good-natured troublemaker around here. Finally, he decided to be honest with the young man in hopes of picking up some more information he could use.

"Your brother brings me here," Boyd said. "I work for the Cattleman's Protective Association, and Jonas Fletcher wrote a letter asking for our help."

Chuck's eyes widened. "You're a range detective?"

"Some people call us that. The Association refers to us as field agents."

Chuck let out a low, admiring whistle and said, "No wonder you're fast on the draw. I'll bet you run into a lot of trouble."

"I see my share," Boyd said. "I imagine you know why your brother called in the Association."

"Those stolen bulls," Chuck said with a solemn nod.

"That's right. Mind if I ask you a few questions about them?"

Chuck shrugged and shook his head. "Go right ahead. Although I don't see how I can help you."

"How long have they been gone?"

"It's been, let me see . . ." Chuck narrowed his eyes in thought. "Two weeks, I'd say, maybe a day or so longer. Jonas saw pretty quick that he wasn't going to get any help from Marshal Durkee or Sheriff Buckston, and the Rangers weren't interested either. So he wrote that letter to your Association right away. I think he was expecting somebody to show up before now."

"I didn't get here in a hurry," Boyd said. "Nobody told me it was anything except a small rustling problem."

"Not really. Those bulls are the only stock anybody around here has lost recently. I guess Jonas didn't explain the situation very well. You have to admit it's sort of odd."

Boyd nodded. Odd was a word he would have used to describe quite a bit about this assignment—including the man sitting on the other side of the table.

"Where were the bulls when they disappeared?"

"In a corral out back of our main barn. Somebody took down part of the fence and led them out in the middle of the night."

"Are you sure something didn't spook the bulls and make them break down the fence themselves?"

"No, the poles weren't busted at all. It was taken down, all right, and by more than one man, looked like."

Boyd nodded. Such a job would require more than one man, that was true. He asked, "Was anybody guarding the bulls?"

"Well, not really. We never thought anything would happen to them, right there so close to the ranch house and all."

"I'm told your brother was asking five thousand dollars apiece for them."

"That's right. He's already gotten half the money too. The buyers are supposed to bring the rest with them when they get here to pick up the bulls." Chuck pulled a heavy pocket watch from his vest, flipped it open, and checked the time. "Which ought to be in about half an hour."

Boyd frowned. "What?"

"The buyers are supposed to arrive today. That's why I'm here in town, to meet them and take them out to the ranch."

"And they've each already paid half the money they owe your brother?"

"That's right."

"What are they going to do when they get here and find out the bulls are missing?"

"Well, that's one of the things that's got Jonas so worried," Chuck said.

Boyd could understand that. After forking over 2500 dollars apiece for some bulls that had mysteriously vanished, the buyers might be tempted to demand their money back and go home. Boyd wondered what sort of a bind that would leave Jonas Fletcher in if it happened. It wasn't surprising that Fletcher was desperate for help from wherever he could find it.

"How are these buyers getting here?"

"A couple are coming in on the evening stage," Chuck replied. "I guess they're planning on hiring some horses and men to help get their bulls back where they're going. The other two are riding in around the same time."

"Each man bought one bull?"

Chuck nodded. "Right."

"Didn't your brother get in touch with them and tell them the bulls had disappeared?"

Chuck grimaced a little and looked off past Boyd's shoulder. He said, "Well . . . no. I think Jonas was hoping he could find the bulls before everybody got here."

There were plenty of other questions Boyd wanted to ask, but at that moment the waitress arrived with a couple of platters loaded with food. Chuck grinned eagerly as the young woman placed plates in front of him.

Boyd was glad the meal had arrived too, and for a few minutes both men were too busy eating to worry about asking or answering questions. The chicken-fried steak was tender and delicious, Boyd discovered, and the potatoes and green beans had just the right amount of pepper in them. The biscuits were light and fluffy, the lemonade cold and tart, with just enough sweetness. The food was as good as any Boyd had had in a while, and he enjoyed it.

He hadn't come to Silver Creek just to partake of the food at the Red Top Cafe, however, and after a few minutes he asked Chuck, "Did you and your brother try to trail those bulls?"

Chuck chewed and swallowed, then said, "We picked up their tracks. Looked like three men hazed them off to the north. We lost the trail after a few miles, though. The ground gets pretty hard and rocky up that way."

"Toward Mike Torrance's ranch, you mean."

"Yeah, that was the way they were headed, all right."

"Do you think Torrance took them?" Boyd asked bluntly.

Chuck hesitated before answering. "I suppose it's possible," he finally said. "Jonas and Torrance have never gotten along very well, and it just got worse when . . ."

"When your niece Belinda and Torrance's boy decided they were in love," Boyd finished.

"Yeah," Chuck admitted. "That didn't make things any better between the JF Connected and the Rocking T. You saw what things are like."

"The fight at Hagen's saloon, you mean?"

"That wasn't the first one. Torrance's riders are mighty proddy these days."

"What started this one?" Boyd asked.

The answer came back too quickly. "Damned if I know," Chuck said vehemently.

Boyd had a feeling Chuck knew more than he was telling about the origins of this particular brawl. The young man could have had something to do with it, Boyd thought. He had already seen how Chuck could stir up trouble. It took a pretty warped sense of humor to come up with the idea of hiding a pig in a parlor where a ladies' sewing circle was about to meet. Maybe Chuck had said or done something to set off the Rocking T punchers.

Or maybe he was innocent this time; it didn't really matter. What was important were those missing bulls—and the buyers who, according to Chuck, would be showing up in Silver Creek at any moment expecting to complete the transaction that had brought them here.

That thought was going through Boyd's head when the sound of horses' hooves and creaking wheels drifted past the batwings on the early evening air. Chuck looked up.

"That'll be the stage," he said. "Guess I'd better get down to the station and greet our guests."

He didn't sound like he was looking forward to the prospect.

Five

Boyd reached for his pocket, intending to dig out some coins to pay for his meal, but Chuck stopped him with an upraised hand. "It's on me," Chuck said as he dropped a greenback next to his plate.

Boyd nodded and said, "Thanks," as he scraped back his chair and stood up. He still had half of a biscuit in his hand, and he took a bite of it as he and Chuck left the cafe.

Chuck turned to the east and went back along the street, past the marshal's office. Hagen's saloon was on the other side of the street. Beyond that on this side of the road was the local stagecoach station, a good-sized frame building with a barn and corrals out back for the switch teams. A large, red-and-yellow-painted Concord coach stood in front of the building, its recent stop indicated by the way it was still rocking slightly on its thoroughbraces as dust drifted through the air around it, and there were quite a few people standing around waiting to see who disembarked. Even though stagecoach traffic was diminishing steadily with the expansion of the railroads, the arrival of a coach was still an occasion for the curious to gather round.

Boyd and Chuck joined the crowd, Boyd swallowing the last of the biscuit as he did so. He leaned against a nearby hitch rail and watched as the jehu swung down from the box and opened the door of the coach. "Silver Creek,

folks," the driver announced to the passengers. "This
here's Silver Creek."

The first person out of the coach was a woman. Boyd
found his eyes drawn to her. Even in the twilight, the
honey-colored hair under the stylish blue hat shone
brightly. Her traveling outfit, though somewhat dusty, was
still elegant. She was on the shady side of thirty, Boyd
decided, but very attractive nonetheless, with the sort of
mature beauty that didn't take itself too seriously.

She was followed from the coach by a second woman,
this one a little older and definitely more plain. She was
also well-dressed, in a bottle-green traveling gown. After
looking around for a moment, she turned and said to
someone still in the coach, "Are you sure this is the right
place, Enos?"

The man who stepped down next from the Concord was
burly and a little above medium height, with long arms and
wide shoulders that stretched the fabric of the dusty black
suit he was wearing. He had rugged features topped by a
black Stetson on gray hair. He nodded and said, "This is
Silver Creek all right, my dear. I've been here before."

"It's not nearly as . . . cosmopolitan as San Antonio, is
it?"

"Not hardly," the man said.

A second man climbed down from the coach. He was
considerably smaller than the first man and wore a brown
suit and a cream-colored Stetson. His dark hair was shot
through with silver. Possessively, he took the arm of the
honey-blonde who had been the first person out of the
stage, and Boyd felt a faint twinge of disappointment. But
he should have expected that a woman so attractive would
be married, he told himself.

The two couples seemed to be the only ones getting off
the stage. Chuck glanced at Boyd, then stepped up to them
and said to the men, "Mr. Clark? Mr. Sumner?"

"I'm Enos Sumner," the bigger of the two men said. He

nodded to the woman next to him. "This is my wife Annabelle."

Chuck snatched his hat off and nodded politely to the woman. "It's an honor to meet you, ma'am," he said. He seemed to have abandoned his normally flippant tone for the time being.

The smaller man said impatiently, "I'm Albie Clark. Did Fletcher send you to meet us?"

"That's right. Jonas is my brother. I'm Chuck Fletcher."

The blonde extended her hand to him and said, "We're so very pleased to meet you, Mr. Fletcher. Or should I call you Chuck? I'm Natalie Clark."

"My sister," Clark grunted.

Well, now, Boyd thought as he straightened away from the hitch rail. That was a little more interesting. He didn't go out looking for women to pursue, not with the memories of Hannah still haunting him. But he could still appreciate a beautiful female when he saw one, and it was a little easier to appreciate them when they weren't married.

Chuck took Natalie's hand and looked like he wasn't sure whether he ought to shake it or kiss it. He settled for giving it a quick squeeze and then dropping it as quickly as possible. He said to Sumner and Clark, "I've hired a couple of buggies for you, and we can start out to the ranch as soon as the others get here."

"There was no one else on the stage with us," Annabelle Sumner said.

"No, ma'am, they're coming on horseback. They didn't have as far to come. Pat Sturdivant's place is over by Jacksboro, and Harry Oliver's spread is on the Brazos near Santo."

"We came from San Antonio," Annabelle said unnecessarily, having already compared Silver Creek unfavorably to the city in South Texas.

"And my ranch is down close to Waco," Albie Clark said.

Boyd wondered when the others—Sturdivant and Oliver,

those were the names Chuck had used—would be arriving.
Dusk was settling down, and although that was a fairly slow
process in Texas in the summer, it wouldn't be long now
until nightfall. Of course, the road leading west out of Silver Creek might be well enough marked to be traveled in
the dark, but Boyd would have preferred seeing the country
for the first time in the daylight.

He was going along with the others when they headed
for the JF Connected, he had decided. Chuck hadn't invited
him, but Boyd didn't intend to wait for an invitation. As
complicated as this case was turning out to be, he wanted
to start untangling the strands of it as soon as possible, and
that meant talking to Jonas Fletcher and taking a look at
the place where the prize bulls had disappeared.

The sound of hooves approaching along the road from
the west made Boyd look around. A middle-aged man,
trailed by a trio of younger men in range clothes, was riding
toward the stagecoach station. The man in the lead was
dressed in the same sort of outfit as the cowboys, and he
sat his saddle with the easy assurance of a man who would
rather ride than walk. As he reined in, he cuffed his hat
back on a shock of snow-white hair and called out,
"Howdy, Chuck."

"Hello, Pat," Chuck greeted the newcomer. He turned
to the others. "Everybody, this is Pat Sturdivant. Pat, I'd
like for you to meet Enos Sumner and his wife, and Albie
Clark and his sister."

"Ladies," Sturdivant said to the two women with a nod.
"Hello, Sumner; howdy, Clark. I hear you boys are here
for the same reason I am."

"Came to pick up a bull," Sumner said.

Chuck exchanged a glance with Boyd, and Boyd read
the look as a plea not to say anything. Boyd gave him a
slow nod, hoping Chuck would take his meaning. Boyd
didn't want to break the news just yet. He'd let Jonas
Fletcher do that. But he *did* want to be on hand when
Fletcher told these folks that the animals they had come to

Silver Creek to buy were no longer anywhere to be found.

"I passed Harry Oliver on the way into town," Sturdivant went on to Chuck. "He and his missus ought to be here any time now."

"He brought Sarey Beth with him?" Chuck asked.

"Sure. Harry doesn't go many places without her. You ought to know that, Chuck. She was with him at that fandango a couple of years ago when you paid those Mexican ladies of dubious virtue to sneak into Harry's hotel room and surprise him."

"He was surprised, all right," Chuck muttered, "and so was Sarey Beth. She threatened to take a shotgun after me when she found out I was mixed up in that deal."

Sturdivant threw back his head and laughed. "I remember. You're damned lucky she didn't do it too."

"I know, I know," Chuck said with an uncomfortable glance at the Sumners and Albie and Natalie Clark.

Boyd suppressed a grin. It appeared that, like most practical jokers, Chuck's pranks caught up with him and even backfired on him more often than not.

At the sound of a wagon drawing near, Sturdivant hipped around in the saddle and said, "Here comes Harry now. He and Sarey Beth brought some of their crew with them to handle that bull, just like I did."

Albie Clark said, "Mr. Sumner and I will need to hire some hands to help us with our animals. Natalie and Mrs. Sumner are going south on the stage again, but Mr. Sumner and I intend to ride back and travel part of the way together."

"That won't be a problem, will it?" Sumner asked Chuck.

"No, sir. There's plenty of good hands around here, and if need be, Jonas can loan you some of the punchers from the JF Connected." Once again Chuck glanced at Boyd, pleading silently with him to help maintain the facade that everything was all right.

These folks were going to be mighty surprised when they

got out to Fletcher's ranch, Boyd thought.

The wagon that had been approaching rolled to a stop, and in the fading light Boyd saw a rail-thin man hop down from the seat and then turn back to help an ample-bosomed, redheaded woman in a long leather skirt and a slouch hat descend. Immediately, she fastened her gaze on Chuck and said, "You! I told you I'd snatch your ears clean off your head if I ever saw you again, Chuck Fletcher!"

"Yes, ma'am, I know," Chuck said miserably. "But Jonas sent me into town to fetch you folks out to the ranch anyway."

"Would've been just as close to go straight to the ranch," the thin man, whom Boyd took to be Harry Oliver, said. "Closer, in fact."

"I reckon that's right," Chuck admitted, "but Jonas wanted everybody coming in together." He turned to the Sumners and Albie and Natalie Clark. "I'll get those buggies now, and we'll load up your bags."

"Good," Enos Sumner said. "I'm ready to get there."

"I certainly am too," Annabelle added. "This has been a long journey."

Too bad they were all destined to be disappointed, Boyd thought. As Chuck hurried off toward a nearby livery stable, Boyd fell in step beside him and said, "I'm going with you out to the ranch."

"Good," Chuck said with obvious relief. "I was hoping you would. Those folks are going to be upset enough when they find out what's happened, but once they hear that a range detective is already on the job—"

"I'd rather you didn't say anything about that," Boyd cut in.

"What?"

"There's no reason to say anything just yet about me being from the Association. I'll tell your brother, of course, but it might be better if the others didn't know."

"Oh. Sure, I understand. You figure you can investigate better if people don't know who you really are."

"Something like that," Boyd said.

Actually, it was exactly like that. Sometimes it was easier to dig into a case when those involved knew he was from the Cattleman's Protective Association, but often it made his job simpler to keep that fact a secret, at least at first. He went on. "Just tell them I'm an old friend of the family or something. You can't pass me off as a member of your crew, not without anybody out there knowing me."

"Yeah, that's right. Whatever you want, Boyd."

What he wanted was to be back in Oklahoma City with Martha, but that wasn't likely to happen for a while. He would have settled for a drink, but that was going to have to be postponed too. Surely Jonas Fletcher had some whiskey out on the JF Connected. Boyd could wait.

He helped Chuck with the buggies, and when they had led the horses pulling the two vehicles back to the station, the stage had already pulled out. The bags belonging to the four former passengers were stacked on the ground in front of the station. Boyd helped load them.

He felt eyes watching him, and glanced over to see Pat Sturdivant following his actions curiously. "Got a new hand, Chuck?" Sturdivant asked.

"No, this is, ah, just an old friend of ours, Boyd McMasters."

Boyd nodded pleasantly to the group, taking them all in with one greeting. "Howdy, folks."

"McMasters . . ." Sturdivant mused. "There used to be a lawman out in West Texas named McMasters, I recollect."

"Do tell," Boyd said, carefully keeping his face expressionless. Here he was, hundreds of miles away from his old stomping grounds, and he had to run into somebody who'd heard of him.

"Yeah. Any kin of yours?"

"Could be," Boyd said with a shrug. "I've got more relatives than a dog's got fleas."

Sturdivant frowned. "That name's familiar for some

other reason too, but I can't recall what it is.'' He shook his head. ''Oh, well, don't reckon it's important. It'll come to me if it is.''

Boyd lifted one of Mrs. Sumner's bags and placed it in the boot at the back of the buggy. Chances were, Sturdivant was a member of the Association and was thinking of Warren. Many of the ranchers in Texas and the whole Southwest were members, and naturally quite a few of them would have had dealings with Warren at one time or another.

It didn't take long to load the buggies. Harry Oliver helped his wife back onto the seat of their buckboard. They had three cowhands trailing them, just as Pat Sturdivant did. It made for a good-sized group as Sumner and Albie Clark helped the other women into the buggies, took up the reins, and then sent the vehicles rolling out of Silver Creek along with the Olivers' wagon and Sturdivant and his riders. Boyd and Chuck rode in front of the procession, Boyd on the grulla that had brought him down here from Oklahoma City, Chuck on a chestnut gelding he had hurriedly fetched from one of the hitch rails near the stage station. Ahead of them, a faint line of red from the now-departed sun lingered on the horizon.

''You don't mind traveling at night?'' Boyd asked in a quiet voice.

''It's no problem. The road's easy to follow, and so is the trail that branches off to the ranch. And there hasn't been any Indian trouble around here for nigh on to twenty years.''

Boyd nodded. He still wished they were making this trip in the daylight.

But wishes were, for the most part, a waste of time. He knew that from bitter experience. Months of wishing that Hannah was still alive hadn't brought her back—and it never would.

With Chuck beside him and the other visitors to the JF Connected trailing behind, Boyd rode on into the gathering night.

Six

The group was about halfway to the trail that branched off to the JF Connected, Boyd judged, when the shooting started.

The flat crack of a rifle and the high-pitched whine of a bullet ricocheting off something blended together into one ugly, all-too-familiar sound. Instinctively, Boyd pulled his revolver from its holster and looked around quickly, trying to judge where the sound had come from. That was difficult to do, especially at night. Annabelle Sumner let out a scream from one of the buggies, but Natalie Clark didn't cry out in the other one. Her brother Albie ripped some curses, though, as another shot blasted somewhere in the darkness.

Boyd and Chuck wheeled their horses around and rode hurriedly back toward the rest of the group. Boyd still hadn't spotted a muzzle flash, so he kept his eyes scanning the moonlit plains around them as Chuck called out worriedly, "Is anybody hit?"

"We're all right," Enos Sumner answered, his voice harsh and angry. "What the hell's going on here?"

Pat Sturdivant galloped up, gun in hand, his men behind him with their weapons drawn too. "That's what I'd like to know," the rancher snapped. "Who's doin' that shootin'?"

As if in response to Sturdivant's question, there was a

third whip-crack of a rifle shot somewhere out there in the darkness. Instinctively, Sturdivant ducked a little, as did Chuck.

By now, however, Boyd could tell by the sound of the shots that the bullets weren't directed toward them. But there was still the danger of a stray slug or a ricochet, so he said to Chuck, "You'd better get these folks moving again. Head 'em on toward the ranch as fast as you can. I'll bring up the rear."

"Good idea, Boyd," Chuck said. To the others, he went on, "Come on, everybody. Let's get to the ranch!"

Boyd wasn't sure how he felt about Chuck sounding like they were old pards or something, but that was something to worry about later. For now, he moved the grulla to the side of the road and waved the others on. Sumner and Clark whipped up the horses pulling the buggies, and Harry Oliver did the same with his wagon team. The vehicles went by in a hurry, trailed by Pat Sturdivant and the cowhands who worked for Sturdivant and Oliver. Boyd saw that Oliver's redheaded wife had picked up a double-barreled scattergun from somewhere in the wagon and appeared ready to use it as she sat on the seat next to her husband.

No more shots had sounded after those first three, which, come to think of it, had been spaced out almost like somebody was signaling. All across the frontier, everybody knew that three shots, spaced like that, were a signal for trouble and meant for anybody in hearing to come a-runnin'. Boyd frowned and called to Chuck, "I'm going to take a look around. See you at the ranch."

Chuck waved and urged his horse into a run, following the others.

Boyd veered the grulla off the road and heeled it into a trot that carried it up into the rolling hills to the south of the trail. He had decided that was where the shots had come from, although it had been impossible to do more than pin down a vague general direction. The travelers, and the road itself, were soon lost from sight.

He holstered his gun, but rode with his hand on the walnut grip. Every sense, every instinct, in his body was alert for danger. In his line of work—in *both* lines of work he had followed in his life—there was nearly always the possibility of a shot coming out of the darkness and ending his existence. But not if Boyd saw the bushwhacker first. As long as that was the case, it was the other fella who was going to die.

Tonight, though, he didn't see anybody, and no more shots disturbed the stillness of the evening. Once he thought he heard the faint sound of hoofbeats coming from first one direction, then another, but he couldn't be sure about that.

Boyd was about to wheel his horse around and start back toward the road when he spotted a faint glimmer of lights in the distance. He reined in, studied the stars for a moment to orient himself, then decided that the lights were in about the right place to be coming from the headquarters of the JF Connected. One thing about this mostly flat North Texas range land—a man could strike out across it without having to worry about encountering too many physical barriers. There were some gullies and creeks that cut across the terrain, but most of them could be negotiated without much trouble.

Knowing that the others would reach Jonas Fletcher's ranch far ahead of him if he went all the way back to the road, Boyd decided to keep going toward those lights. This way might be something of a shortcut, and there was a chance he would reach the JF Connected about the same time as Chuck and the other travelers.

Sure enough, after half an hour of riding in which the only things that slowed him down were a couple of barbed-wire fences—which luckily had gates in them fairly close by—Boyd was close enough to the ranch headquarters to make out the big, three-story, whitewashed house surrounded by live oaks, as well as the scattering of outbuildings that included a long, narrow bunkhouse, a cookshack, a smokehouse, and several large barns. There were also some spacious corrals beyond the barns, one of which, he assumed, had held the missing bulls before their disappearance.

Boyd was also able to see the road in the moonlight, and he spotted Chuck moving along it toward the lighted buildings, along with the other riders, the two buggies, and the wagon. That was good timing, Boyd thought. He heeled the grulla into a little faster pace.

Chuck was just reining to a halt in front of the big house when Boyd rode out of the shadows and into the yellow glow that washed out from the lanterns on the front porch. "Boyd!" he exclaimed. "Where'd you come from?"

"Took a shortcut," Boyd replied curtly.

"Did you see who was doing that shooting?"

"Never saw anything," Boyd said. "I thought I heard a couple of people on horseback once, but I never spotted them."

He swung down and followed Chuck's example, looping the reins of his horse over a hitch rack that stood before the ranch house. The buggies and the wagon were just coming to a halt nearby.

In a low voice, Boyd said to Chuck, "You'd better pass the word to your brother who I really am, since I'm pretending to be a friend of the family. We don't want him giving anything away."

"Yeah, right." Chuck hurried up the four steps onto the broad wooden veranda just as the door of the house opened and a man stepped out. Chuck leaned close to the man's ear and said something in a voice too low for even Boyd's keen ears to make out the words. The man nodded, then came to the edge of the porch, standing at the top of the steps with his hands tucked into the back pockets of his denim pants.

He was a well-built man of middle years with a tanned, open face and close-cropped, dark blond hair that was starting to turn gray. He called out in a friendly voice, "Well, hello, Boyd. Good to see you again. Next time let us know you're coming and I'll send somebody into town to meet you.''

Boyd heard the faint edge of irritation in the man's voice, although it was concealed well. He stepped up onto the porch and took the hand Jonas Fletcher stretched out to him. ''Chuck took care of that,'' Boyd said. ''Since he was meeting these other folks, he just brought me along too.''

Fletcher's eyes narrowed slightly. ''We'll have to have a nice long talk later, catch up on old times.''

''I'm looking forward to it,'' Boyd told him.

Fletcher moved past him and went down the steps to greet the others. Enos Sumner was helping his wife down from their buggy, and before Fletcher could say anything, Annabelle turned to him and said loudly, ''We were attacked!''

''Attacked?'' Fletcher repeated in surprise. ''What happened?''

''Bandits, I think. Dozens of them! They were all shooting!''

''Now, Annabelle,'' her husband growled. ''It wasn't quite like that.'' To Fletcher, Sumner said, ''Somebody took a few shots with a rifle. I couldn't tell if they were aiming at us or not, but nobody was hit.''

Pat Sturdivant dismounted and chimed in. ''Didn't sound to me like they was tryin' to bushwhack us, Jonas. The shots took us by surprise, but none of 'em came close.''

Sarey Beth Oliver brandished her shotgun from the wagon seat. ''If anybody had tried to stop us, I was ready for 'em! They'd've said howdy to a load of buckshot!''

''Well, I'm sorry to hear that there was trouble of any sort,'' Fletcher said, raising his voice a little to address all of the newcomers. ''Pat, Harry, your boys can go on out to the bunkhouse. The rest of you come inside. I want to hear all about it.''

Boyd and Chuck stood to one side, waiting as Fletcher led the others into the house. Quietly, Boyd said, ''Good job. Your brother picked right up on the way I wanted it.''

"Jonas will go along with whatever you want, I expect . . . as long as you get results."

Boyd grunted.

He and Chuck took off their hats as they followed the others inside. They had gone into a parlor that was furnished with thick rugs on the floor, low sofas, and heavy armchairs. A massive fireplace, unlit now in the heat of summer, took up almost an entire wall. An assortment of weapons were hung on pegs driven into the wall above the fireplace, mostly long guns ranging from an old flintlock musket to the most recent model of Winchester. Boyd also saw a couple of old Paterson Colts hanging in a place of honor. He wondered if the heavy, long-barreled revolvers had been carried by one of the ancestors of Jonas and Chuck, one of the patriarchs of the Fletcher family. The guns, the fireplace, and the furnishings all gave the room a decidedly masculine look.

Fletcher turned to face his guests and said, "First of all, I haven't had the pleasure of meeting a couple of these ladies."

"This is my wife Annabelle," Sumner said as he put his arm around the woman's shoulders. She still seemed shaken by the experience along the road.

Fletcher nodded politely to her and murmured a greeting. Before Albie Clark could introduce his sister, Natalie stepped forward and took care of that chore herself. "I'm Natalie Clark," she said as she held out a gloved hand to Fletcher. "I've heard so much about you from my brother, Mr. Fletcher."

He took her hand and smiled. "Please, call me Jonas."

"Why, certainly. And I'm Natalie."

She was flirting with Fletcher the same way she had behaved toward *him*, Boyd thought. Obviously, it was just her nature, something that started up whenever she was around men. He had known some women like that in the past.

Sarey Beth Oliver came up to Fletcher and flung her arms around him. "You know me, you old hoss-thief!"

she boomed. "Good to see you again, Jonas!"

"And it's always good to see you too, Sarey Beth," Fletcher replied, sounding a little breathless from the hug she had given him.

"You better make sure that brother of yours steers clear of me, though," she went on, turning serious and giving Chuck a cold glance that made the young man fidget and look away. "I ain't forgotten what he did at that party a couple of years ago."

"None of us have, Sarey Beth. I promise you that Chuck won't be a bother this time. Will you, Chuck?"

Chuck shook his head rapidly. "I'll behave, Jonas. You've got my word on it."

Sarey Beth Oliver snorted. "See that you do, boy."

Pat Sturdivant cuffed his hat back and rubbed his hands together. "Where are them bulls, Jonas?" he asked. "I know it's sort of late—"

"Too late to do anything about it tonight," Jonas said quickly. "We'll talk business first thing in the morning. Right now, I've got a spread all laid out for you folks in the dining room. Come with me."

"I hope there's nothing that will disagree with my digestion," Annabelle Sumner said. "I'm afraid this trip has been so difficult that my poor delicate stomach is easily upset."

"I'm sure it'll be fine," her husband said to Fletcher. "Come along, Annabelle."

Natalie Clark linked her arm smoothly with Fletcher's. "Lead the way, Jonas," she said with a smile.

Boyd and Chuck brought up the rear as the others moved from the parlor into a large dining room. This room showed the same masculine influence as the parlor, with its long, heavy table and several sets of steer horns mounted on the walls. There was also a fireplace in the dining room.

Boyd wondered if Jonas Fletcher was a widower. He might have taken the man for a lifelong bachelor if he hadn't known that Fletcher had a child. But from the looks of things, Fletcher's wife—Belinda's mother—had been either dead or gone for a long time, long enough so that any mark she had made on this dwelling had disappeared.

For that matter, Boyd suddenly asked himself, where was Belinda Fletcher? Shouldn't she have greeted her father's guests too?

The table was set for company, and it was loaded down with platters of food. Boyd saw ham and roast beef and fried chicken, potatoes and greens and black-eyed peas and pinto beans. Several plates of cornbread were just waiting for butter and honey, and condensation dripped down the sides of pitchers filled with buttermilk cooled in a well, more than likely. It hadn't been that long since Boyd had eaten at the Red Top Cafe in Silver Creek, certainly not long enough so that he needed another meal, but the food looked and smelled so good that he found himself growing hungry anyway.

Jonas Fletcher bustled around, playing the host and seeing that his guests were seated comfortably. A couple of Mexican women emerged from another room and started serving the food. Boyd and Chuck were still standing to one side, and after he was satisfied that everything was going smoothly, Fletcher moved over to join them and said in a low voice, "I'm glad you're here, Mr. McMasters. Why don't you and Chuck come with me into the office?"

Boyd nodded. "Good idea."

Fletcher said to the others, "You folks go right ahead and enjoy your meal. I'll be back shortly. Just a little business to discuss."

"I thought you said it was too late to talk business," Albie Clark said sourly.

"Well, some things won't wait," Fletcher said.

"This is quite a surroundin', Jonas," Sturdivant put in. "You go ahead. I reckon this'll keep us busy for a while."

"Thanks, Pat." Fletcher led the way out of the dining room through another door, Boyd and Chuck following him. As soon as they were out of sight of the others, the jovial expression dropped off of Fletcher's face like a stone. He looked as grim as a man regarding his own grave.

"I hope you're damned good at your job, McMasters," he grated as he shut the door of a cluttered, book-lined office behind them. "Otherwise we're all liable to be up Shit Creek."

Before Boyd could make any reply to that, a high-backed chair that was placed behind a massive desk, facing the other direction, swiveled around and a female voice said, "Oh? And just whose fault is that, Daddy?"

Seven

Fletcher's face darkened ominously. "Damn it, Belinda, what are you doing poking around in here?"

The young woman stood up from the chair where she had been sitting, her back to the door, until Boyd, Fletcher, and Chuck had come into the room. "I'm not poking around in anything, Daddy," she said. "I was just sitting here."

And doing it beautifully, Boyd would have wagered. She was an exceptionally attractive young woman, with long, dark-brown hair parted in the middle, olive-skinned features with an exotic loveliness set off by the small birthmark on her right cheek, and a slender but well-curved body displayed to advantage by an open-throated white shirt and a fawn-colored riding skirt. She must have inherited her good looks from her mother, because Boyd saw only the slightest resemblance to either Jonas Fletcher or Chuck, just enough to know that she was related to them.

He saw something else too as she came out from behind the desk. Her boots were dusty, as was the hem of her skirt.

Like she had just come in from riding?

Fletcher said, "This is a private discussion, Belinda," but she ignored him and moved closer to Boyd.

"Who is this?" she asked bluntly.

"My name's Boyd McMasters," he told her.

"He's an old friend of the family," Chuck put in.

Fletcher snapped, "Damn it, that story's for the rest of them, Chuck. Belinda knows better."

"I should say so," the young woman went on. "I wouldn't have forgotten such a handsome man. I'm pleased to meet you, Mr. McMasters."

Belinda Fletcher evidently had some of the same flirtatious streak that Natalie Clark had displayed earlier. Boyd wasn't sure he liked that. Too many women who were too friendly had a tendency of muddying up the waters during an investigation.

On the other hand, it was flattering to have women like Natalie and Belinda showing an interest, even if it didn't mean anything.

Jonas Fletcher moved behind the desk and sat down in the chair his daughter had been occupying. "McMasters is from the Cattleman's Protective Association," he said as he took a cigar from a box on the desk.

"Oh!" Belinda exclaimed. "A range detective."

"Field agent," Boyd said, feeling like he had had this conversation too many times in the past.

Belinda shrugged prettily. "It doesn't matter what you call it. You're still here to find Pestilence, War, Famine, and Death, aren't you?"

Boyd didn't know how the hell to answer that, but he didn't have to. Fletcher banged a fist down on the desk and said, "Damn it, those aren't their names! They're bulls. How can you name them for the Four Horsemen of the Apocalypse?" He looked at Boyd in exasperation. "Never educate a female, McMasters. Not unless you're prepared to be frustrated all the damned time."

"All right, all right," Belinda said. "Call them whatever you want. What's important is that they're missing."

"Because of that damned young buck who wants to come sniffing around here after you!"

Belinda swung toward her father and said angrily, "Griff had nothing to do with stealing those bulls! I've told you—"

"You won't believe anything bad about that son of a bitch, but I know his father, and the apple doesn't fall far from the tree."

Chuck said, "It couldn't, could it? I mean, gravity pulls the apple straight down, so it's got to be close—"

Boyd said, *"Shut . . . the hell . . . up!"*

All three of them stared at him.

He took a deep breath and went on. "I used to drink more than I should, and this whole business is making me think I've backslid and started imagining things again. Chuck, sit down and be quiet. Miss Fletcher, you too." He turned toward Fletcher. "Now, tell me what happened, and we'll figure out what to do about it."

Fletcher put the unlit cigar in his mouth and clamped his teeth down on it. "I don't take kindly to people talking to me like that in my own house, mister."

"I don't mean any offense," Boyd said. "I just want to get to the bottom of this. That's what I was sent here to do."

Fletcher sighed and said, "I reckon you're right. Belinda, you can stay if you want, but let Mr. McMasters and me talk. Chuck . . ."

Chuck held up his hands. "I'll butt out, Jonas."

Fletcher gestured at the chair in front of the desk. "Have a seat, McMasters. I'll fill you in."

Since Fletcher hadn't offered him a cigar, Boyd took out one of his own Primeros as he settled himself in the chair. Chuck took a ladderback chair, reversed it, and straddled it, while Belinda sank into an armchair in front of some of the bookshelves. She watched with an intent, still-angry expression on her lovely face as her father and Boyd lit their cigars from a kitchen match that Fletcher scraped into life.

Fletcher blew smoke into the air and said, "It's pretty simple, really. I had four of the most valuable young bulls in this part of the country, and somebody stole 'em. I figure Mike Torrance and that son of his are behind it."

"But you don't have any proof," Boyd said, speaking quickly to forestall any protest from Belinda.

"I don't have any proof," Fletcher said with a shrug. "But I know Torrance would like nothing better than to see me ruined, especially since I told that boy he'd get a load of buckshot in the seat of his pants if he kept coming around here and bothering Belinda."

"Griff wasn't bothering me," the young woman said bitterly. "We're in love."

Fletcher snorted. "You're too young to know anything about love."

"Mother was younger than I am now when she married you," Belinda pointed out. "And she wasn't much older when she left."

Fletcher's teeth clenched on the cigar, and his face turned a deep shade of red. "I've told you not to talk about that," he grated. "It doesn't have anything to do with what's going on now."

Boyd cocked his right foot on his left knee. He wasn't too sure that Fletcher was right . . . but the plain and simple fact of the matter was that his brother Warren had sent him here to find those stolen bulls, not to hash out what was evidently the troubled past of the Fletcher family. He said, "Chuck told me somebody stole the bulls from one of your corrals."

Fletcher was still glowering at his daughter. He looked away from her and nodded. "I'll show you the place in the morning. It was pretty obvious from all the tracks what had happened. Several men came up to the corral during the night, took down some of the rails, and drove the bulls off. We tried to track them, but the bastards were too slippery."

"What did you do then?"

"Took some of the boys and rode straight up to the Rocking T," Fletcher growled. "I told Mike Torrance flat out I wanted my bulls back. He claimed he didn't know what I was talking about, told us to get off his range pronto or he'd have his men ventilate us."

"I thought there was going to be shooting for sure," Chuck put in.

Fletcher put his cigar aside and said, "I didn't want to get any of my men killed, so we pulled out. But I'm still convinced that Torrance is behind the theft."

To Boyd's way of thinking, that was possible—but it didn't have to be the only possible explanation. He said, "You were selling all four of the young bulls, right?"

Fletcher nodded. "You met the buyers. All four of them put up half the money for the bulls, and they've got the other half with them now. All that's left is to turn the bulls over to them."

"Which you can't do."

"Which I can't do," Fletcher agreed, his jaw taut with anger and frustration. "They'll be well within their rights if they all demand that I return their money."

"And you don't want to do that."

"Of course not," Fletcher said without hesitation. "Running a ranch is an expensive proposition. The place needs a little infusion of cash every now and then."

"Don't we all," Boyd muttered as he leaned forward in his chair. "You've stalled the buyers tonight. What are you going to tell them in the morning?"

"Well . . . I thought about telling them that the bulls are out on the range and will have to be rounded up. . . ."

"That won't put them off for more than a day. It looks to me, Mr. Fletcher, like you're going to have to tell them the truth."

"Including the fact that you're an agent from the CPA?"

Boyd sighed. "If you have to. I was hoping to keep that quiet for a while, but I reckon that's going to be hard to do."

"I don't like this. I don't like it a bit."

"Neither do I," Boyd said. "But since the timing brought us all here at once, there doesn't seem to be any getting around it."

Fletcher nodded slowly. "All right. I'll go ahead and

break the news to them in the morning. Pat Sturdivant and Harry Oliver are old friends of mine; they'll give me some time to recover the bulls before they start asking for their money back. But I don't know Sumner and Clark as well. I'm not sure what they'll do.''

"Maybe you can talk them into waiting before they do anything.''

"What's your first move going to be?''

"Too much time has passed to track the bulls themselves. That trail is too cold by now. But I can start poking around some, maybe spook whoever is responsible for taking the bulls into making a move that will lead me to them.''

"You'd better start at Torrance's place,'' Fletcher suggested.

"You'll be wasting your time if you do, Mr. Mc-Masters,'' Belinda put in coldly. "Griff and his father didn't have anything to do with this. I know.''

"We'll see, miss,'' Boyd told her mildly. He didn't want to get drawn into what was obviously a long-standing argument between Belinda and her father. He pushed back his chair and stood up. "Now, if you don't mind, I could use some sleep. I had a long ride today.''

"We've got plenty of spare rooms,'' Fletcher said, "even with all the company on hand. Chuck, take Mc-Masters upstairs and get him settled in.''

"Sure, Jonas,'' Chuck replied as he stood up. "Come on, Boyd. We'll get your gear from your horse and I'll show you where to bunk.''

Chuck led him out of the room, and as he left Boyd threw one last glance over his shoulder. Belinda Fletcher was still pouting, and he was willing to bet that she would light into her father again as soon as they were alone.

He couldn't help but wonder . . . if Belinda *had* been out riding just before everybody else reached the ranch, what had she been doing gallivanting around in the dark? Could her errand have had anything to do with those mysterious rifle shots?

Boyd was too tired to think about it overmuch. He retrieved his saddlebags and the big .70-caliber rifle from the grulla, and Chuck promised to have one of the ranch hands tend to the horse. "It'll be in the barn if you need it," Chuck promised.

As they went up a set of back stairs to the second floor of the big house, Boyd asked, "You think you could have one of those women bring up a plate of food for me? Seeing all that spread got me a little hungry again."

"Me too," Chuck said with a grin. "I'll see to it, Boyd." He led the way down a corridor with a carpet runner in the center of it, pausing to open a door near the far end of the hallway. "This room ought to suit you just fine."

Boyd stepped inside, saw a comfortable-looking bed, a dressing table with a pitcher of water and a wash pan on it, and a couple of chairs. A lamp was lit on a side table, and curtains fluttered gently in the breeze that came in through an open window. The breeze was beginning to cool off a little after the heat of the day, but the air wouldn't really be cool until just before dawn the next day, Boyd knew. Not in Texas at this time of year.

He pitched his saddlebags and rifle onto the bed and nodded to Chuck. "You're right, this'll do me. Thanks."

"Say, Boyd," Chuck began, then hesitated. Finally he pointed at the rifle and went on. "What kind of gun is that? I don't reckon I ever saw one quite so big."

"It's a .70-caliber. I did some modifying on it myself, so I guess you could say it's one of a kind." Boyd picked up the weapon, jacked the lever, and caught the unfired cartridge that was ejected. As he showed it to Chuck, he said, "I did some modifying on the bullets too."

Chuck's eyes widened. "What's that shoved into the snout of that slug?"

"It's a carpet tack," Boyd said grimly. "When it hits

something, the tack makes the slug split apart and mushroom out.''

"Good Lord," Chuck breathed. "That'd put a hole the size of a cannonball through a man, or take an arm or a leg right off.''

"That's the general idea. It only takes one shot from this rifle to kill a man, no matter where I hit him.''

Chuck frowned. "You wouldn't be showing this to me because you've got the idea that I, ah, sort of like to play jokes on people every now and then, would you?''

Boyd smiled humorlessly and said, "I'm not much of a man for jokes.''

"Neither am I. Not anymore. Good night, Boyd.''

"'Night, Chuck. Don't forget about that food.''

"No, sir!''

The door slammed behind Chuck, and Boyd gave a genuine chuckle as he slipped the shell back into the rifle and placed it carefully in a corner. He probably shouldn't have buffaloed Chuck like that, he thought, but at least now he wouldn't have to worry about snakes in his bed or any other sort of foolishness.

Boyd hung his saddlebags over the foot of the bed, unbuckled his gun belt and draped it over one of the posts on the headboard, then stripped off his shirt. He turned toward the pitcher and the basin, eager to wash off some of the trail dust, when a soft knock sounded on the door. That would be the servant with his plate of food, he thought. Over his shoulder he said, "Come in.''

The door opened, and Belinda Fletcher said, "Well, Mr. McMasters, it didn't take long for you to become rather informal, did it?''

Eight

Boyd spun around in surprise. He had been expecting one of the heavyset, middle-aged *mamacitas* he had seen in the dining room downstairs, not this young, dark-haired, dark-eyed lovely. But Belinda had a plate in her hand, and it was piled high with ham and beans and cornbread.

"Uncle Chuck said you were hungry," Belinda went on with a sweet smile as she came into the room. She passed closely by Boyd as she went to the dressing table to set the plate on it. He smelled a faint, clean scent and knew it was uniquely hers.

"I wasn't expecting you to bring the food," Boyd said.

Belinda shrugged, making even that simple gesture graceful and somehow sensuous. "I saw Consuela on her way upstairs with the plate, so I took it and said I'd bring it to you."

A warning bell as strident as any that hung in a firehouse was going off in the back of Boyd's mind. The case that had brought him here to Texas was proving to be a lot more complicated than he had expected, and he didn't need the further distraction of this little minx. He said in a flat voice, "Thanks for the food, Belinda, but you'd better go now."

She had turned to face him, and her eyes were boldly exploring his rangy, well-muscled torso. She said, "I was hoping we could talk a while first."

"About what?"

"Those missing bulls." The flirtatious look disappeared from her face as she went on hurriedly. "Griff didn't have anything to do with stealing them, Mr. McMasters, and neither did his father. I'm sure of it."

So, Boyd thought, the seductive attitude was just an excuse so that she could plead the case for her boyfriend's innocence some more. Some men might have been disappointed by that; he felt only a surge of relief. He sure as hell hadn't wanted to have to fight her off tonight.

"Look, Belinda," he said, "my job's to find out what happened to those bulls and get them back for your father if I can. If Griff and Mike Torrance are involved in that, then it's their own lookout."

She came a step closer. "You don't understand—"

"I reckon I do. You figured you could sashay in here, distract me with how pretty you are, and convince me to leave the Torrances and the Rocking T out of my investigation. Sorry, but it's not going to work."

Her features hardened, becoming a little less lovely—but only a little. "Men are more stubborn than those damned bulls!" she burst out. "You make up your mind and then there's no changing it."

"I haven't made up my mind about anything, except that I want to eat that snack and then get some sleep," Boyd told her firmly. "If Mike Torrance and his boy didn't have anything to do with stealing those bulls, they've got nothing to worry about from me."

"I wish my father had never even bought that first bull!" She spun and headed for the door.

Boyd let her go. She was convinced of the innocence of Griff and Mike Torrance, that was clear. But she was also in love with Griff Torrance, and love had the power to blind people to some of the most obvious things. All emotions, when they were strong enough, shared that power.

Boyd knew that all too well.

He sighed, picked up the plate, sat down in one of the chairs, and began to eat. The food didn't taste as good as he had expected it to, and weariness was settling in around his shoulders.

But it would be morning soon enough, and then he could get to work.

"What the hell did you say?" Albie Clark exploded.

His sister caught at his sleeve. "Now, take it easy, Albie," Natalie said. "I'm sure Jonas didn't mean that like it sounded."

"I'm afraid I did," Jonas Fletcher said grimly. "The bulls aren't here."

The entire group was seated around the table this morning for breakfast, including Boyd and Chuck. A place was set for Belinda too, but she hadn't come downstairs yet and it didn't appear that she would be doing so any time soon. Boyd lifted a cup of black, steaming, excellent coffee and sipped from it as the confused muttering spread around the table and turned into a full-fledged uproar.

Everyone's plate was empty except for the one in front of Annabelle Sumner, who had only picked at her food. Jonas Fletcher pushed his plate away from him a little and stood up, raising his hands for quiet. Gradually the questions, which were starting to turn angry, died away.

"I know I should have explained this last night," Fletcher said, "but I figured you were all tired from your trips and it would be better to wait until morning."

Pat Sturdivant asked, "What happened to them bulls, Jonas?"

"Someone stole them," Fletcher replied bluntly.

That declaration led to more surprised questions from everyone around the table. Boyd caught Fletcher's eye and cleared his throat, and Fletcher held up his hands again, waiting until the others had settled down.

"Folks, you met Boyd McMasters last night, but I'm afraid I didn't tell you the truth about him. He's not an old friend of the family. He's really a field agent from the Cattleman's Protective Association."

"A range detective!" Albie Clark exclaimed.

Boyd closed his eyes for a second and sighed. Then he pushed his chair back and stood up. "That's right," he said. "I've been sent here to find out who stole those bulls and get them back for Mr. Fletcher . . . and for you folks who are buying them."

Sturdivant slapped a callused palm down on the table. "I knew I'd heard that name before. There's a fella called McMasters who's some sort o' high muckey-muck in the CPA, ain't there?"

"My brother Warren," Boyd acknowledged. "He's the vice-president—and my boss. He's the one who sent me to Silver Creek."

"This is intolerable," Enos Sumner rumbled. "I put up half the money for that bull in good faith, and now I'm told that it's gone, that it's been stolen or some such."

"There's no 'or some such' about it, Enos," Fletcher said, his voice hardening a little. "I've told you the truth about what happened. If you think this is some sort of trick, or some attempt on my part to swindle you . . ."

"No, no," Sumner said quickly, holding up his hands. "I didn't mean it like that, Jonas. But you've got to admit, news like this can throw a man for a loop."

Fletcher nodded curtly. "Of course. It certainly threw me for a loop when I discovered that the bulls were gone. But I can promise you, we're going to get them back."

"How can you make a promise like that?" Albie Clark demanded. "How long have they been gone?"

"About two and a half weeks," Fletcher admitted.

Clark snorted in disgust. "Hell, they could be in Canada by now! Or in some slaughterhouse."

Boyd said, "Nobody's going to slaughter bulls that are worth so much money, and whoever took them had to know they were valuable. I'm a little surprised the thief hasn't gotten in touch with you, Mr. Fletcher, and demanded some sort of ransom."

Fletcher shook his head. "Nothing like that has happened."

Natalie spoke up, saying, "Well, I think we should give Mr. McMasters a chance to investigate. If anyone can get those bulls back, it's him."

"How do you know that, Natalie?" her brother asked. "You don't even know this man McMasters."

She turned and smiled at Boyd. "I know him well enough to tell that he's intelligent—and tough. Aren't you, Mr. McMasters?"

"I just try to do my job," Boyd said. "And I reckon I'd better start by taking a look at the corral where those bulls were being kept when they disappeared."

Several of the others stood up too, and Fletcher said quickly, "Can I count on all of you being patient? If you'll give us a few days, I'm sure we'll have the bulls back."

"You're being mighty optimistic, if you ask me," Clark said. He went on grudgingly. "But I suppose I can wait a day or two and see if this range detective turns up anything."

"I'll wait a while," Sumner said, sounding as reluctant as Clark.

Sturdivant said, "You know you can count on me, Jonas."

"And Harry and me trust you, Jonas," Sarey Beth Oliver put in. It occurred to Boyd that he hadn't heard Harry Oliver say more than half-a-dozen words since the man had arrived at the ranch. Evidently he was accustomed to keeping quiet and letting Sarey Beth do the talking for both of them.

Since Boyd hadn't worn his revolver to the breakfast table, he excused himself for a moment and went upstairs to fetch it. He was buckling on the gunbelt as he stepped out into the hall again, and as he did so, one of the doors farther along the corridor opened and Belinda Fletcher emerged from the room. She was wearing a dressing gown and her hair was tousled from the bed. Boyd thought she looked beautiful.

She just gave him a cold stare, however, so he merely nodded, said, "Good morning," and went quickly to the staircase. Fletcher and Chuck were waiting for him at the bottom of the stairs.

Fletcher led the way out the back door of the ranch house. They passed the parlor, where Boyd saw Annabelle Sumner and Natalie Clark sitting on one of the low sofas. The four buyers, along with Sarey Beth, were waiting outside. Obviously, they had invited themselves to come along as Boyd began his investigation.

The whole group walked over to the first barn. Double doors were open in front and back of the big building, allowing a breeze to blow through it. As Boyd walked through the barn with the others, for a moment the distinctive smells of dust and straw and shit made his mind go back to his own ranch, the ranch he had owned when he was still the sheriff of Reeves County—and when Hannah was still alive.

Doing his best to ignore the flash of pain, Boyd pushed the memory out of his head. He was a long way from West Texas and his old life, and he had a job to do.

The large, spacious, now-empty corral behind the barn was sturdily built, but a few experienced men could have taken some of the rails down without too much trouble. Twenty thousand dollars worth of prime breeding stock was enough to make quite a bit of trouble worthwhile. As Jonas Fletcher slapped a hand on one of the rails and said, "This is the place," Boyd looked at the gate that was built into the corral fence. A heavy padlock hung in the hasp that held the gate closed.

"Was that gate locked the night the bulls were stolen?" he asked.

Fletcher nodded. "That's right. I guess they figured it would be easier—not to mention quieter—to take down some of the fence rather than try to bust that lock."

"Who's got keys to the lock?"

"I do, of course," Fletcher said. "And Chuck, and there's a spare in the house."

"But an outsider wouldn't have been able to get hold of a key without either breaking into the house or taking one off you or your brother."

"That's right."

Boyd nodded slowly. He looked at the ground. There was a welter of boot tracks and animal prints in the dust. "What could you tell from the sign the next morning?"

"Not much," Fletcher said. "There were several men, but it was impossible to be sure just how many. I reckon they all had horses, though, and when they had the bulls out, they started them moving north, circling around the ranch buildings until they were clear."

"And nobody noticed anything was wrong?"

There was a touch of exasperation in Fletcher's voice as he replied, "The bulls were in a locked corral no more than a hundred yards from the house. Nobody expected any trouble. There hadn't been any rustling around here to speak of in years. Silver Creek's a pretty peaceable place—except for those damned Rocking T riders. They're troublemakers, every single one of 'em, but what else could you expect when they ride for the likes of Mike Torrance!"

Boyd ignored that. The hostility between Fletcher and Torrance might well have played a part in this, but Boyd didn't want to leap to any conclusions without some evidence to back them up.

"How far were you able to follow the tracks?"

"A couple of miles. They veered off into a rocky stretch this side of the main road, and we lost them there. We went on across the road and checked up and down for several miles, trying to see where they crossed, but we never found anything. The bastards were smooth. It's not like they were pushing a whole herd. The tracks of four bulls and a few horses wouldn't be that hard to wipe out."

Fletcher was right. It was damned difficult to cover the

tracks of an entire herd, which was why it was relatively easy sometimes to track down rustlers. But when the stolen animals were so few in number . . .

Enos Sumner asked, "What do you think, McMasters?"

"It's too soon to think anything," Boyd told him. "I'm still looking. That comes first." He turned to Fletcher again. "I'm going to saddle my horse and have a look around your spread."

"Chuck had better go with you," Fletcher said. "That way my punchers will know it's all right for you to be riding on JF Connected range. We're all pretty edgy right now. Wouldn't want somebody taking a shot at you just because they didn't recognize you."

"Sure, I'll be glad to go with you, Boyd," Chuck said eagerly. "Say, maybe I can help you with your investigation. I've read a bunch of those Old Sleuth and Nick Carter dime novels."

Boyd tried not to wince. While he had to admit it was probably a good idea to have Chuck accompany him, he wasn't looking forward to being saddled with the young man's "help." It looked like Chuck intended to trade in being a practical joker for a new interest—detective work.

And he had come down here to look into a simple little case of rustling, Boyd thought with a sigh.

When he got back to Oklahoma City, Warren was sure as hell going to get an earful about *this* one.

Nine

Under other circumstances, it might have been a pleasant morning. Enough fluffy white clouds floated in the blue, arching Texas sky to cover the sun from time to time and keep the heat from building up too rapidly. It had been a wet spring in these parts, and even though the usual summer dry spell had already set in, the grass was still lush and green in most places. Boyd and Chuck rode over rolling hills and across wide meadows, passing stands of live oaks and little creeks lined with towering cottonwoods.

"Looks like a nice spread," Boyd commented about an hour after they had left the ranch house. "You and your brother must have worked hard to build it up."

Chuck nodded. "Jonas, mostly. He's always been the one who wanted to keep growing and making the place better. It was just a little homestead with less'n a hundred cows when our pappy died and left it to us. *His* pappy— our grandpap—settled up here in this area not long after Texas gave up being a republic and joined the Union. It's good range land for the most part . . . sandy loam in the bottoms, black clay up on the higher ground. Plenty of farming in this area too, but it's still cattle country."

"You and Jonas own the place equally?"

Chuck looked surprised by the question. "Well, yeah, I guess we do. But he's always run things, and that's fine by me. I never wanted to be the one calling the shots."

Boyd was watching the other man intently without appearing to do so as Chuck answered the question. It had occurred to Boyd that Chuck might resent his brother being the boss on the JF Connected, right down to using his own initials to devise the ranch's brand. But Chuck's lack of interest in being in charge seemed to be genuine, as far as Boyd could tell.

They rode in ever-widening circles around the ranch headquarters, taking their time so that Boyd could get a feel for the place. The terrain became more rugged the farther west they went; the hills rolled a little more, some of them topped with rock-littered ridges. Finally, Boyd reined in and said, "Show me where you lost the tracks of those bulls."

"Sure." Chuck pointed to the northeast. "It's off that way."

So far the young man had surprised Boyd by not asking a lot of questions about his past or about other cases on which he had worked. He didn't expect Chuck to restrain his curiosity forever, though, and sure enough, as they cut across the ranch toward the spot where the trail had disappeared, Chuck said, "What's it like, being a detective? I've never been anything but a cowhand."

Boyd thought for a moment, then said, "Being a field agent for the Association is just as boring as being a cowhand most of the time, I reckon, and sometimes just as dangerous. I spend a lot of time riding the range, just looking at things."

"But you get to track down rustlers and capture criminals. Sounds to me a lot like being a marshal or a Ranger."

Boyd shrugged. "Some of the work is like carrying a law badge, sure. The best part about it is not being tied down to any one place for too long. I ride in, do my job, and move on. That's the way I like it. I guess I'm just a drifter at heart."

"I've never been any farther than Waco. The Association's offices are up in Oklahoma City, aren't they? That's a big town."

"It's grown a lot in the last couple of years," Boyd agreed. "I don't care for it that much."

"I'd still like to see it. They've got some tall buildings in Fort Worth and Dallas now. Skyscrapers, they call 'em, just like the ones back East. Progress is coming quick to this part of the country."

Boyd looked out over the landscape through which they were riding, and thought that although Chuck was right about the spread of progress throughout the Southwest, you couldn't really tell it by looking. This part of the country looked pretty much the way it had looked fifty years earlier when it was still roamed by Comanches and Kiowas. One of these days, though, folks were going to wake up and find that the frontier was gone, stolen away while they weren't watching. Some people would welcome that.

Boyd wasn't so sure he would. . . .

They pushed on and reached the rocky stretch where the tracks of the stolen bulls had vanished. As Boyd reined in and studied the ground in front of him, he could understand why it had been impossible to follow the trail any farther. What appeared to be a huge, subsurface rock some two or three miles wide had evidently been forced up by some seismic upheaval in the dim past, so that the clay had been displaced by a flat, pebbly floor of limestone. The area was about half a mile wide, Boyd judged, and ran as far as he could see to right and left. He rode out onto the rock, and the grulla's shoes rang loudly against the hard surface.

"Looks like there would've been at least a few marks left by the hooves of the bulls and the shoes of the horses," he mused as he looked down at the rock.

"Well, if there were, we couldn't follow 'em," Chuck said. "We'd have needed an Apache tracker with us."

Boyd nodded and lifted his gaze. He could see the road that led to the settlement of Silver Creek in the distance, beyond the massive flat rock. "They drove the bulls across here, then along the road," he said.

"Yep, that's what we figured. And we never found where they left the road, even though we went up and down it for miles. Like Jonas said, those ol' boys were pretty slick."

Boyd didn't like to admit it, but he knew that Chuck was right. The thieves had known what they were doing. It would have been difficult enough to find them if he had come along the next morning. Now, with a trail that had been growing colder and colder for more than two weeks, the chore was going to be even worse.

That just meant he would have to look closer, prod harder . . . outthink the thieves. It would be a challenge—but Boyd figured he was up to it.

"Let's go see Mike Torrance," he said.

Chuck gave him a dubious frown. "I was sort of afraid you might say that. They don't take kindly to anybody from the JF Connected riding on Rocking T range."

"I'm not one of your brother's hands."

"Torrance may not see it that way. After all, you're working for Jonas right now."

"I'm working for the Cattleman's Protective Association," Boyd said curtly. "If you don't want to go with me, Chuck, I reckon I can find the way myself."

"Oh, I'll go with you," Chuck said. "Jonas expects me to give you a hand, and besides, I want to see how you handle Torrance. But don't be surprised if the reception we get up there isn't very friendly."

"I'm not interested in making friends, just in finding answers."

Boyd heeled the grulla into a trot that carried it across the rock toward the road, and Chuck, riding a chestnut gelding, fell in beside him. When they reached the road, they turned back to the east and followed it for a mile or so before reaching the trail that ran north to the Rocking T.

"You're sure about this?" Chuck asked as they paused.

"I'm sure," Boyd said with a nod. "If Torrance is responsible for the theft, I want him to know that I'm going to keep digging around until I can prove it. Then maybe he'll be spooked into doing something that'll just give him away that much sooner.''

Chuck frowned again. ''Sounds sort of like painting a bull's-eye right on your back.''

''I told you the job could be dangerous sometimes.''

As they rode toward the headquarters of the Rocking T, Boyd saw that the range up here, while not as outstanding as on the Fletcher spread, was still quite good. The cattle he and Chuck passed were mostly longhorns, and when Boyd commented on that, Chuck replied, ''Mike Torrance has always said that the old ways are good enough for him. His father and grandfather raised longhorns, and he's not interested in trying to bring in any other kind of stock.''

''Then he wouldn't have taken those bulls for breeding purposes, to try and improve his herd?''

Chuck shook his head. ''The only reason he'd have for stealing the bulls would be to cause trouble for Jonas.''

Boyd ventured on to a subject he hadn't raised yet with Chuck. ''What about your niece? Is Belinda really in love with Griff Torrance?''

Chuck looked like he wished Boyd hadn't asked him that question. ''I've always tried to steer clear of Belinda's problems.''

''She's had a lot of trouble, has she?''

''Well, her ma—Jonas's wife Sally—she left when Belinda wasn't much more than a baby. Ran off with a traveling man from Houston who she'd met in Silver Creek. She left a note telling Jonas not to come after her or try to find her. Sally never did care much for living on the ranch. She wanted to see what life in the big city was like. Can't say as I blame her for that.''

''Abandoning her husband and her child . . . that's pretty rough. What did Jonas do?''

''He went after her, even though she'd asked him not to. Left our old *segundo,* Cap Parsons, to run the ranch while he rode out on their trail. I asked Jonas to take me with him—I was almost twenty, and I figured I was old enough to go along—but he wouldn't do it. He just took a few of our hands.''

Chuck fell silent, and after a few moments, Boyd asked, "Did he ever find her?"

"Nope," Chuck said with a shake of his head. "He never did. And I was never sure if I was happy or sad about that. I always got along just fine with Sally, and I missed her a lot after she was gone, but I can't help but think she was happier somewhere else. I hope so, anyway.''

Boyd nodded slowly, saying nothing. More than likely, he thought, either Sally Fletcher had gotten tired of the drummer she had run away with, or he had gotten tired of her, and Sally had wound up working in some saloon or crib, living a miserable existence that had ended at an early age. That was the way those fairy-tale romances usually wound up on the frontier, and happily-ever-afters were damned rare.

But they had been known to happen, Boyd supposed, and he told himself to stop being so blasted cynical. Anyway, Jonas Fletcher's troubled marriage didn't have anything to do with those stolen bulls.

A few minutes later, they came within sight of the Rocking T headquarters. The ranch house itself was older, a large double cabin with a dogtrot in between, built of logs that had been roughly hewn into thick, massive beams. The bunkhouse and the barns and the storage buildings were of more recent construction. Boyd and Chuck reined in at the top of a rise to study the place, which was located in a small valley in front of them. A creek ran about fifty yards behind the cabin, and several towering pecan trees grew between the stream and the ranch house. Boyd saw several men moving around the barns.

"You intend to just ride in there?" Chuck asked, sounding a little nervous.

"I intend to just ride in," Boyd said firmly.

Before he could get the grulla moving again, however, several riders emerged from a stand of oaks about a hundred yards away. The horsebackers moved rapidly along the ridge toward Boyd and Chuck.

"Oh, *hell*!" Chuck said, the exclamation heartfelt. "That's Mitch Riley in the lead."

Boyd rested his hands on the saddlehorn and studied the oncoming riders. He remembered Riley's name from the day before, and he vaguely recognized the man. It took a moment for full recollection to come to him, though.

When it did, he smiled humorlessly and said, "That's the gent whose toe got shot off in the saloon yesterday."

"The gent whose toe *you* shot off, you mean," Chuck said. "And I'd be willing to bet he's still not very happy about it."

Chuck was right about that. Boyd didn't have any doubts on the matter.

Especially when, a moment later, Riley whipped a rifle from his saddle boot and spurred into a gallop toward them, firing as he came.

Ten

It was a good thing, Boyd thought, that the hurricane deck of a running horse was such a piss-poor platform for accurate shooting. Some of the slugs plunked into the ground yards ahead of Boyd and Chuck while others screamed far overhead. None of the rifle bullets came anywhere dangerously close to them, however.

Boyd unshipped his revolver and pulled the grulla's reins taut. The horse was threatening to shy. Beside Boyd, Chuck exclaimed anxiously, "Damn! What're we going to do?"

Short of turning tail and running—something he didn't want to do—Boyd didn't see that they had any options other than waiting for Riley to come within handgun range and then blowing the proddy son of a bitch out of the saddle. But he was saved from having to do that when one of the other men, none of whom were shooting, galloped up alongside Riley and reached over to wrench the barrel of the rifle down.

"Hold it, Mitch!" Boyd heard the man yell. "What the hell do you think you're doing?"

The other riders came up even with Riley as the hothead reined in abruptly, sawing brutally at his horse's mouth with the bit. Boyd and Chuck stayed where they were, watching with great interest as Riley glared at the man who had just put a stop to the shooting. "Damn it, Griff, this is personal!'' Riley exploded. "You got no right to horn in like that!"

Boyd looked over at Chuck and asked quietly, "The youngster is Griff Torrance?" Chuck nodded without saying anything.

Griff pointed a finger at Riley and said, "You ride for the Rocking T, Mitch, and when my pa's not around, that means you ride for me! And I say we don't try to gun down guests on our range, no matter who they are!"

"Guests!" Riley threw back at him. "Those ain't guests! One of 'em's that grinnin' hyena Chuck Fletcher, and the other is the bastard who shot my toe off yesterday!"

"That still doesn't give you leave to start slinging lead at them. I'll talk to them, find out what they want here." Griff looked at the other hands. "I'm counting on you boys to keep Mitch from making a fool of himself, hear?"

There were nods of grudging agreement from the cowboys gathered around Griff and Riley. They didn't look any too happy to see Boyd and Chuck either, but at least they weren't blazing away at the two visitors. Griff wheeled his horse, a good-looking buckskin, and rode the twenty yards or so that separated the others from Boyd and Chuck.

"Howdy," he said as he drew rein in front of them. "Hope you fellas have a good reason for being here."

"I'm just along for the ride, Griff," Chuck said. "It was Mr. McMasters here who wanted to come have a talk with your daddy."

Griff studied Boyd for a moment, and Boyd returned the scrutiny. Griff Torrance was a handsome young man in his early twenties, slender but muscular, with tanned, lean features and sandy brown hair worn longish over his ears and down the back of his neck. He wore range garb like the other men, but his saddle was a little fancier than most of those ridden by forty-a-month-and-found cowhands. That was the only indication that he was the son of the Rocking T's owner and not one of the spread's punchers.

"McMasters, eh?" he said. "What's your business here,

Mr. McMasters? Or did you come just to gloat over shooting off Mitch's toe?''

"That idea never entered my head,'' Boyd replied honestly. "When I decided to ride over here, I never even
thought about running into Riley. Truth is, I'd just about
forgotten about what happened yesterday.''

The other men were close enough to overhear Boyd's
answer, and Riley howled, "Forgot about it! You wouldn't
forget, you son of a bitch, if it was your foot hurtin' like
blazes all night!''

Boyd looked over at the angry cowboy and nodded
coolly. "You're right, I reckon I wouldn't. But it didn't
seem like a very good idea to just stand there and let you
gun down the marshal either.''

Griff shot a hard glance at Riley. "You said the fella
who shot you threw down on you for no reason, Mitch.
What's this about trying to gun Marshal Durkee?''

Riley grimaced as he said, "Aw, hell, McMasters
must've saw it all wrong.''

"Yeah. I reckon.'' It was clear from Griff's tone of voice
that he didn't believe Riley. He looked back at Boyd.
"Don't push your luck, mister. Mitch doesn't like you, and
none of us care much for Chuck here. So you'd better answer my question. What are you doing here?''

"I came to talk to your father,'' Boyd said. "That's what
I intend to do.''

Without warning, he heeled the grulla into motion. Griff
gave ground, backing his horse out of the way, then looked
angry with himself for doing so. Boyd didn't look at the
Rocking T cowboys, but he heard the angry mutters and
knew that some of them were likely resting their hands on
their gun butts right about now. Chuck jogged his horse
alongside him and said nervously, "Uh, Boyd . . .''

"Come on,'' Boyd snapped. "We came here to ask questions, not answer them.''

A moment later, Griff's buckskin moved up on Boyd's
other side. With grudging admiration in his voice, the

young man said, "I'll give you this much, Mr. Mc-Masters—you must have the balls of a brass monkey."

"Hell, no," Boyd snorted. "What good would that do?"

Griff didn't have an answer for that, and in fact he looked vaguely embarrassed. Boyd kept riding down the gentle slope toward the big log cabin that housed the head-quarters of the Rocking T, flanked by Chuck and Griff. The other men trailed along behind them.

A couple of huge mutts emerged from the dogtrot and began barking loudly as the riders approached. A moment later, a man came out of the right-hand side of the cabin and shouted, "Bear! Buffalo! Shut up, you mangy curs!" The dogs slunk around the corner of the cabin as the man faced the oncoming riders, his hands clenched into fists and propped on his hips.

He was a medium-sized man but carried himself with an air of strength and confidence. There was nothing cocky or arrogant about it, just calm and self-assured. Although he was middle-aged, his hair was still thick and dark. He wore a leather vest over a hickory work shirt, and there was a holstered six-gun strapped around his hips.

"You're not welcome here, Chuck Fletcher," he called as the riders came to a halt in front of the cabin. Boyd heard a trace of an Irish accent in his words, but it was faint, almost overwhelmed by the drawl of a longtime Texan.

"I know that, Mike, but Mr. McMasters here wanted to talk to you, and I told Jonas I'd come along too."

"What, that brother of yours is afraid I'd murder a man out of hand?" Torrance squinted at Boyd. "Even a man who'd blow the toe off one of my best men?"

"If a hothead like Riley's the best you've got, Torrance," Boyd said, "maybe you'd better give some thought to hiring some new men."

Behind him, Riley said, "That does it!"

Boyd didn't turn. Torrance held a hand up, making a curt gesture, and Boyd knew that if Riley was reaching for a gun, that gesture would have stopped him. Mike Torrance had the look of a man who was accustomed to being obeyed, instantly and completely.

"I know your name's McMasters," Torrance said. "I know you took a hand in that fracas in Silver Creek yesterday. Now state your business here on the Rocking T."

"That's a matter that ought to be discussed between you and me, Torrance. If you'd ask me to get down off this horse . . ."

Under his breath, Chuck muttered, "You don't get down off a horse, you get down off a . . ."

He shut up when Boyd glanced at him, the CPA man's eyes as cold as chips of ice.

Torrance waved his hand impatiently. "Sure, get down. Come inside. Have a drink even. I'll not have anyone saying that Mike Torrance isn't a hospitable man."

"Boss!" Riley sounded aggrieved. "You can't mean you're goin' to drink with this—"

"That'll be enough out of you, Mitch Riley," Torrance snapped. "Get on back to work, all of you. Griff, come inside with us." He added as an afterthought, "You too, Chuck."

Boyd swung down from his horse, as did Chuck and Griff, and along with Torrance they stepped into the shade of the dogtrot. Torrance led the way inside the cabin.

The place had a puncheon floor, and a woven rug thrown down in front of the fireplace added a bright splash of color to an otherwise drab room. Like the Fletcher house, there was no sign of a feminine hand here. Chuck had mentioned earlier as they were riding that Torrance was a widower and had been for quite a few years.

Torrance took a jug from a cabinet and uncorked it. "Irish whiskey," he said with a touch of belligerence as he thrust the jug toward Boyd.

Boyd said, "That's the only kind, isn't it?" and enjoyed the brief look of surprise on Torrance's florid face. He took the jug and tilted it to his mouth, downing a long swallow despite the fact that it wasn't yet noon. It hadn't been too awful long since Boyd had stayed drunk just about all the time, morning, noon, and night. He didn't have any trouble swallowing the raw, fiery liquor now.

He used the back of his other hand to wipe his mouth as he passed the jug back to Torrance. "Smooth," he said.

Torrance gave him a shrewd look. "And so are you, I'd wager, Mr. McMasters. Now, who the hell are you, and what are you doing here?"

Boyd told the truth, saying, "I ride for the Cattleman's Protective Association. I'm here to find out who stole those young bulls from Jonas Fletcher and get them back for him if I can."

"I knew it!" Griff said angrily. "Fletcher's still got a burr up his ass about us and those damned bulls!"

Torrance shot his son a hard glance. "Watch your language, boy. This was your mother's parlor, and don't you forget it." He took a little nip from the jug, then faced Boyd again. "Jonas told you I stole those bulls, did he?"

"He figures you might've had a hand in it," Boyd said evenly. "Did you?"

The blunt question prompted Torrance to blink and then take another slug of whiskey. He said harshly, "I don't normally let a man waltz into my home, drink my whiskey, and then accuse me of being a goddamned thief!"

"I'm not accusing you of anything. I just told you what Jonas Fletcher thinks—which you already knew—then asked if there was any truth to the charge."

Torrance snorted in contempt. "As if you'd believe me if I said I didn't have a blessed thing to do with those bulls disappearing."

"I might," Boyd said. "I came here with an open mind, Torrance. Convince me."

"Why the hell should I take the time and trouble to do that?"

"Because I'm going to find out who stole those bulls sooner or later." Boyd didn't allow the slightest doubt to creep into his voice as he made the statement. "You can make things easier for me by eliminating yourself and your son as suspects."

For a moment, Torrance didn't say anything. Griff stood to one side, still looking angry, and Chuck fidgeted a little, his gaze going back and forth between Boyd and Torrance. Both men looked as stubborn and immovable as the North Texas hills.

"Why in blazes would I even *want* those bulls?" Torrance finally demanded. "Texas longhorns are good enough for me, just like they were good enough for my father and his father, just like they'll be good enough for Griff there when I'm gone. Ain't that right, boy?"

"That's right, Pa," Griff said. Boyd didn't think he sounded completely sincere, however.

"Nobody claimed you took the bulls to improve your herd," Boyd said. "You couldn't breed them with your stock, not right out in the open, since everybody in these parts probably knows about Fletcher losing the bulls. Next year's calf crop would look mighty suspicious if they weren't pure longhorn, since I suspect most folks know how you feel about that too."

"Damn right they do," Torrance growled.

"But there'd be nothing stopping you from stealing the bulls and selling them somewhere else," Boyd went on. "Maybe you need money. Maybe you've got a note coming due at the bank and you're short on cash. Hell, maybe you just want to embarrass Fletcher because he doesn't like the idea of your son courting his daughter."

Griff spoke up again, exclaiming, "Leave Belinda out of this! She doesn't have anything to do with it!"

Torrance motioned for his son to be quiet. Slowly, he said to Boyd, "Now that's a mighty far-fetched theory, mister."

Boyd shrugged. "Not any more far-fetched than Griff and Belinda falling in love, considering how you and Fletcher feel about each other. I'm surprised you'd give the romance your blessing, but that's what I've heard.''

"Belinda's the only one of those Fletchers who's worth a damn,'' Torrance said. He glanced at Chuck and added, "Present company included, unfortunately.''

Chuck's jaw tightened. Even the most easygoing of the Fletchers had a hard time ignoring an insult like that, Boyd thought.

But before Chuck could make any retort, Boyd went on. "You know Jonas Fletcher has some buyers at his place now, ready to pick up those bulls?''

"I heard as much,'' Torrance admitted. "I even know a couple of 'em, Pat Sturdivant and Harry Oliver. They must be pretty upset this morning.''

"Nobody down there on the JF Connected is very happy,'' Boyd said. "But the buyers are willing to give Fletcher a little time, and I intend to have those bulls back where they belong before too much longer.''

"Got an idea where they might be, eh?'' Torrance asked mockingly.

Boyd just smiled confidently and didn't say anything.

He watched Torrance closely, but he wasn't surprised when he saw little or no reaction from the cattleman. Torrance's weatherbeaten face was like stone when he wanted it to be, revealing nothing of what went on behind his eyes. After a few seconds, Torrance said, "You'll take no offense if I don't wish you luck, I suppose.''

"No offense,'' Boyd said. "And there'll be no hard feelings if I find out you stole the bulls and I turn you over to the county sheriff or the Rangers?''

Torrance's breath hissed between clenched teeth. "Damn you, McMasters,'' he grated. "I've taken all of you that I intend to. I want you out of my house and off my land as soon as you can manage it.''

Chuck plucked at Boyd's sleeve. "He means it, Boyd.''

With an irritated shrug, Boyd pulled away from Chuck. "I know that. But he knows I mean it when I say I'm going to find those bulls. Don't you, Torrance?''

Torrance didn't answer. Instead, Griff stepped between the two men and said tightly, "My father told you to get out. You may be tough, McMasters, but you can't fight everybody on the whole damned ranch."

"No, he certainly can't," Chuck said quickly, "and neither can I. Come on, Boyd."

"All right," Boyd said slowly. "We're going, Torrance. But I'll be back if I find anything pointing me toward you as the thief who took those bulls."

Torrance's face, which seemed to be flushed most of the time anyway, was growing darker and redder. Boyd swung around, confident that he had pushed Torrance, and the situation, as far as he could afford to for now. He walked toward the door, Chuck hurrying along beside him.

Torrance and Griff both came out into the dogtrot to watch them mount up and ride away. Some of the Rocking T hands were idling around near the cabin, and out of the corner of his eye, Boyd saw them start toward the corral where their horses waited. One of the men limped heavily, so Boyd had no trouble identifying him as Mitch Riley.

"Oh, shit!" Chuck said fervently. "They're going to come after us. We'd better light a shuck—"

"Wait a minute," Boyd cut in.

A moment later, Torrance called out, "Damn it, I told you boys to get back to work. Leave those horses in the corral and get on about your business."

Chuck looked back over his shoulder and heaved a sigh of relief. Then he glanced over at Boyd. "How'd you know Torrance would stop them?"

"He didn't strike me as the kind of man who'd let somebody else avenge an insult. He took the things I said— and the things I implied—personal. If there's a score to settle, he'll settle it personal."

"You think he'll try to bushwhack you?"

Boyd smiled thinly. "If he does, I'll know why. If he's just mad—but innocent—he'll do it face-to-face. Back-shooting means he *does* know something about those missing bulls.''

Chuck sleeved sweat from his forehead. "I've changed my mind, Boyd. I wouldn't want your job, wouldn't want it at all."

Nobody bothered them as they rode back toward the main trail. When they reached it and had left Rocking T range, Chuck gave an even bigger sigh.

"Didn't know if we'd ever make it off that spread alive," he said. "Let's get back to the house. We ought to make it about lunchtime."

"You go ahead," Boyd told him. "I'm going to ride into Silver Creek."

"What for?"

"Just a couple of errands to run." Boyd turned the grulla toward the east and lifted a hand in farewell.

"Boyd!" Chuck called after him. "Need me to come with you?"

"Nope."

"Well . . . you be careful," Chuck said. As Boyd rode away, he heard the other man mutter, "Damned target on his back . . ."

That was just about right, Boyd thought.

Now he had to wait and see who drew a bead on it.

Eleven

Boyd kept his eyes moving as he rode toward Silver Creek, remembering the warning from Marshal Durkee about how the Rocking T and JF Connected cowboys liked to take potshots at one another across the road. He didn't see any other riders, though, until he was closer to town, and they appeared to be farmers, rather than cowhands. He passed a couple of wagons too, each of them carrying a farm family and loaded with produce that was evidently bound for the public market in Silver Creek.

When he reached the settlement, he spotted the marshal walking along the main street and raised a hand in greeting as he drew alongside Durkee. "Morning, Marshal," Boyd said.

Durkee squinted up at him. "You still alive?"

Boyd swung down and fell in step beside Durkee, leading the grulla by the reins. He asked, "Why wouldn't I be?"

"Figured Mitch Riley would've shot you by now. He was tellin' everybody in town who'd listen last night that he was goin' to, next time he saw you."

Boyd decided not to give Durkee the satisfaction of admitting that Riley had tried to do just that. Instead, he said, "Do I look shot to you?"

"Nope. Maybe a mite frazzled around the edges, though.

Any luck findin' out who stole those bulls from Jonas Fletcher?''

"Not for sure. There are enough hard feelings between Fletcher and Mike Torrance, though, that I can understand why Fletcher blames him.''

Durkee nodded. "Those two don't get along, that's for damn sure. Never have. Things might've been different if Evelyn and Sally had both been around. They were good friends, the short time Sally was married to Fletcher.''

"Evelyn was Torrance's wife?''

"That's right,'' Durkee said. "And a finer woman never lived in these parts. But she was a plain-spoken woman, and the way I heard it, she told Sally Fletcher that she had to follow her heart. Well, Sally followed it, all right—as well as followin' that fella from Houston.''

Boyd frowned. What Durkee had told him added yet another wrinkle to the long-standing feud between Jonas Fletcher and Mike Torrance. It was entirely possible that Fletcher blamed Evelyn Torrance for encouraging his wife to run off with that drummer. Evelyn had passed away, though, which could have led Fletcher to transfer his resentment to her husband, adding to the ill feelings that already existed between the men.

That was pure-dee interesting—but it didn't bring him any closer to the stolen bulls.

"Where's the nearest place somebody could have sold those bulls?'' he asked.

"The Livestock Exchange down in Fort Worth, of course,'' Durkee snorted, as if anybody would know that. "You think the thief sold 'em instead of keepin' 'em?''

"Everybody around here knows about the bulls being stolen,'' Boyd pointed out. "Don't you think that if somebody was hiding them, some talk about it would have leaked out by now?''

"Well, maybe,'' Durkee admitted. "Silver Creek's gettin' to be a good-sized place, but it's still small enough so that it's hard to keep a secret for too long.''

"And yet you haven't heard any rumors about the bulls, have you?"

Durkee shook his head. "Nope. 'Course, I ain't been tryin' to dig up any rumors neither. That'd be your job, Mr. Range Detective."

Boyd reined in the irritation he felt at the irascible lawman. He said, "Fort Worth's pretty close. I'm not sure the thief would feel safe trying to sell the bulls there."

"Well, there's markets over in Weatherford and Mineral Wells, and up in Jacksboro. Hell, the fella's had time to take 'em all the way out to Eastland or Cisco, or clear down to Waco."

Boyd nodded. Unfortunately, what Durkee said was true. Any sane man might look at this case, decide the trail was too cold, and give up.

Luckily, sanity wasn't something he'd been accused of overmuch, especially in recent years.

"Thanks, Marshal. You reckon you can point me to the Western Union office?"

"It's down yonder in Morrison's Drug Store, in the back corner. Morrison doubles as the key-pounder. He's got one of them telephone things too, got a line goes right into Fort Worth. Only one in this part of the county."

"No, thanks." Boyd shook his head. "The telegraph will do fine for what I need."

With a casual wave, he parted company with Marshal Durkee and headed toward the drugstore the lawman had pointed out. It was a white, two-story frame building on the west side of the street, a few doors down from the cafe where Boyd had met Chuck the day before. A narrow staircase on the outside of the building led up to the second floor, and a sign at the bottom of the steps announced that the IOOF lodge met up there.

Boyd had done some thinking on the way into town, and he had decided to send a wire to his brother requesting information on the four men who had come to the JF Connected to purchase the missing bulls. While he couldn't come up with any logical reason for Sturdivant, Oliver, Sumner, or Clark to be involved with the theft, knowing as much as he could about everyone connected to the case could come in handy. He was going to ask for all the information Warren could dig up on Jonas and Chuck Fletcher too. He wanted to know just how badly it was going to hurt Jonas if the rancher had to return the money that had already been paid to him for the bulls. Since it was likely all the men were members of the Cattleman's Association, Warren ought to be able to find out quite a bit about them, Boyd thought.

His boot heels rang on the plank sidewalk in front of the drugstore. He opened a screen door and went inside. The place was laid out like a hundred others he had seen. Shelves full of patent medicines in dark brown bottles lined the walls; glass-topped counters containing candy and notions were in front of the shelves; and in the center of the room, also surrounded by a counter, was a soda fountain. Just inside the door, on the front wall underneath the window, was a short set of shelves where several rows of dime novels were displayed, their garish yellow covers competing for the eye of potential readers. In one of the rear corners, just as Durkee had said, an alcove had been built in, with an opening left in one of the walls to serve as a window for the customers. Through the opening, Boyd could see the array of telegraphic equipment, as well as the large wooden box on the wall with a black speaking tube curving out from it. The box also had a black earpiece hanging in a sort of cradle on one side, and the other side had a crank on it. That was the telephone, Boyd knew. He had seen them before, even talked on one a time or two. But he didn't like them, and regarded them with the same sort of suspicion with which many Indians looked at cameras. There was something unnatural about being able to talk to somebody whose voice was there while their body could be dozens—or even hundreds—of miles away.

A couple of youngsters were seated on revolving stools

at the soda fountain, and several women were browsing at the glass-topped counters. A man in a white shirt, vest, bow tie, and stiff collar was standing behind the sofa fountain counter, polishing glasses with a cloth. He had a stiffly waxed handlebar mustache, and he called out to Boyd, "Good day to you, sir. What can I do for you?"

"You'd be Mr. Morrison?"

"Yes, sir, indeed I would."

"I need to send a wire," Boyd said.

The drugstore owner/telegrapher pointed to the walled-off alcove. "If you'll go back there and print out your message, sir, I'll be with you momentarily."

Boyd did as Morrison asked, finding yellow telegraph blanks and a pencil on a small shelf built below the window in the alcove. With quick, firm strokes, he printed what he wanted to send, and by the time he was finished, Morrison had entered the booth by way of the door and was waiting for the message. Boyd pushed it across the shelf to him.

"This is a pretty long message," Morrison said with a slight frown. "It'll cost a bit to send, sir."

"That's all right," Boyd assured him. The Association would wind up paying for it.

Morrison counted the words, collected the fee, and then sat down at the key to tap out the message. Boyd wandered around the drugstore in the meantime, listening with one ear to the rapid-fire series of dots and dashes from Morrison's key. He recognized enough Morse code to know that the druggist was sending the message correctly. Some of these small-town key-pounders had been known to make mistakes.

When he was done, Morrison came to the window and asked, "Will you wait for a reply, sir?"

"No, it's liable to take too long. I'm staying at the JF Connected. Can you send somebody out there with the reply when it comes in?"

"Certainly," Morrison replied.

Boyd gave the man an extra dollar for his trouble, then

walked out of the store. He didn't want any licorice whips or sodas or vitality tonics.

Or maybe he should have gone for one of those tonics after all, he thought fleetingly as he stepped out onto the sidewalk and ran smack into Natalie Clark. A man needed vitality for an experience like that.

"Oh! Mr. McMasters!" she exclaimed. "I didn't see you."

"Sorry, ma'am," he said, reaching up to touch a finger to the brim of his hat. "Reckon it was my fault. I wasn't watching where I was going."

"Well, that's understandable," she said with a smile. "After all, you have a great deal on your mind, I would imagine, what with trying to find those stolen bulls and all. I know it's only been a few hours, but have you made any progress?"

"Not really," he admitted. He didn't want to discuss the case with her, so he changed the subject by saying, "I didn't expect to run into you here in town."

"One of Jonas's men drove me in. I needed to do a bit of shopping." She lifted the bag she was carrying. "A lady tends to run out of things on a long journey, you know."

They began walking side by side along the street. Boyd said, "You and your brother came up here from Waco, is that right?"

"Yes, that's where Albie's ranch is. Well, not in Waco itself, of course, but on the Brazos River northwest of town."

Boyd nodded. "Pretty country. I've been in that neck of the woods a time or two."

"We like it."

"Does your husband work with your brother on the ranch?"

Natalie lifted a gloved hand and shook a finger at him. "Now, Boyd, you know good and well I'm not married. You don't have to go fishing like that. I'm sure an observant man like you—a detective, for heaven's sake—has already noticed that I'm not wearing a wedding ring."

Boyd grinned. "Well, I guess I *did* happen to notice that, all right."

"Since you know I'm a shameless unmarried woman, I'm going to be bold and ask you to have lunch with me."

"I knew about the unmarried part," Boyd said. "I didn't know anything about you being shameless."

She smiled at him. "You will," she said sweetly. "Oh, yes, I think you will."

Despite Natalie's flirting, nothing improper happened during lunch, which they ate at the Red Top. Boyd had steak and potatoes again, while Natalie ordered baked chicken and a salad. "A woman has to watch her figure, you know," she explained.

Boyd refrained from saying that he enjoyed watching her figure, but from the look in her eyes, he figured Natalie knew what he was thinking.

The peach cobbler Chuck had eaten the day before had looked mighty good, Boyd recalled, and since the menu chalked onto a blackboard on the wall announced that the cafe had Brazosberry cobbler today, he ordered a couple of bowls of them. Natalie had to be persuaded that one bowl of cobbler wouldn't ruin her figure, but when she began eating, she shared Boyd's opinion that the pie was delicious.

As they were lingering over the last of the cobbler, Natalie brought up the subject of the missing bulls again. "What are you going to do now?" she asked. "It seems like it would be awfully difficult to locate any clues after this long."

"That's true," Boyd admitted, "and to be honest, I haven't decided what my next move is going to be. But I can tell you one thing: I'll find those bulls sooner or later."

"My, you sound awfully determined."

"The Association pays me to solve the cases they send me out on. I've always figured if a man signs on to do a job, he'd damn well better do it, pardon my French."

Natalie smiled. "Don't mind about that, Boyd. Goodness, Albie can make the very air turn blue around his head when he's upset about something . . . which is more often than I'd like, I must say."

Boyd heard a faint sigh in her voice, and he said, "Well, it did strike me that your brother was a mite short-tempered."

"That's putting it mildly. But he's always taken care of me—or we've taken care of each other, I guess you could say—and I don't know what I'd do without him."

"A smart, beautiful woman like you . . ." Boyd shrugged. "I reckon you'd make out just fine."

"Well, thank you, kind sir. I'd like to think you're right."

They finished their pie, drank the last of their coffee, and left the cafe after Boyd settled up with the waitress. Natalie offered to pay for her part of the meal, since, after all, she had invited him, but Boyd shook his head firmly.

"I suppose I should be heading back to the ranch now," Natalie said as they strolled down the street toward the livery stable where the buggy had been left.

"I can ride with you," Boyd offered.

"Oh, that's not necessary. I've already taken up enough of your valuable time, Boyd."

"It's no bother."

"Tell me the truth," she said. "Were you planning to ride back out to the ranch now, or were you going to stay in town longer?"

Boyd hesitated, then did as she asked and told her the truth. "I was going to poke around a little more here in town."

"Then I think that's exactly what you should do. I've got Jonas's man to drive me back out there." She stopped and put a hand on Boyd's arm, tilting her head a little to look up into his eyes. "But if you'd care to take me riding some other time . . ."

"I'll take you up on that," Boyd said without hesitation.

"Good." She squeezed his arm. "I'll see you later then."

Natalie turned away and started toward the livery stable again. Boyd watched her go, enjoying the graceful yet sensuous way in which she moved. He was trying to force his brain off of Natalie's lovely figure and onto the case at hand when someone ran hard into his back.

Boyd spun, every instinct in his body crying out that he was under attack. His hand flashed to the gun on his hip as he took a quick step backward, trying to put some distance between himself and whoever had jumped him. His hand closed around the butt of the revolver.

But he wasn't being attacked, he realized suddenly. The person who had run into him was a young woman, and as he stopped himself from drawing the gun, she clutched at his shirt and turned a sobbing, tightly drawn face up to him.

"Oh, my God!" she said in a quavery half-scream. "You've got to help him! Somebody's got to help him!"

"Who?" Boyd demanded.

The young woman, who had tangled blond hair and heavy, smeared makeup, wore a robe hastily wrapped around her, despite the fact that it was a little past the middle of the day. Instead of answering Boyd's question, she grabbed his arm, pointed down the alley from which she had doubtless just emerged, and said raggedly, "He's back there! My God, I think somebody's killed him!"

Warning bells were still going off in Boyd's brain. This could be a trap of some kind. But the young woman might be telling the truth. There might actually be a wounded man back there in the alley who needed help. Boyd couldn't stand by and not find out for sure.

Palming out his gun and holding it tightly, he plunged into the alley, the distraught young woman at his heels.

Twelve

It wasn't a trap. Boyd knew that as soon as he saw the man sprawled around the corner of the building, right outside a rear door that hung open. The man was lying on his back, staring sightlessly up at the pale blue Texas sky.

His throat had been cut, damned near from ear to ear.

Boyd stopped short at the gruesome sight. The young woman bumped into him from behind again and asked breathlessly, "Is he . . . is he . . ."

Boyd looked at the dark pool of blood that had flowed from the man's slashed throat and puddled around his head, where it was now soaking into the dirt of the alley. "I'm afraid so," Boyd said. He turned toward the young woman and she came into his arms, burying her face against his chest and beginning to sob.

He felt awkward as all hell standing there, his left arm around the woman's shoulders, still holding the gun in his right hand. Holstering the weapon while there was a murdered man lying at his feet didn't seem like a very good idea, though, so Boyd hung on to the revolver.

There was no doubt in his mind this was murder. The worst drunk in the world couldn't have cut his throat like that by accident; Boyd felt well qualified to make that judgment since he himself had been well on his way to that designation before finally sobering up. Nor would the man have done it on purpose. Anybody wanting to do away with

himself could have found an easier, quicker method—
although it was doubtful this man had lived very long once
the blood began to pump out through the gash in his neck.

"Who is he?" Boyd heard himself asking.

"His . . . his name's Lonnie," the woman said between
sobs. "He's . . . he was a customer of mine."

Boyd had already figured her for a soiled dove. No other
kind of woman would be wearing that much makeup and
a dressing gown at this time of day. He looked at the par-
tially open door and asked, "Is that your room?"

"Y-yeah. Lonnie was . . . my last customer last night. He
paid for . . . for the rest of the night."

"Why don't you go inside and sit down, so you won't
have to look at this?" Boyd suggested. "I'll fetch the marshal."

She clutched at his arms. "Do you have to?"

Boyd glanced again at the bloody corpse. "Don't see any
way around it, I'm afraid."

She sighed, then nodded. "But hurry. I . . . I feel better
when you're around, mister."

Normally Boyd would have taken such a statement for
whore talk and put about as much stock in it as it deserved.
But this young woman was much too shaken to be doing
anything except telling the truth. He steered her toward the
door, gave her a little pat on the rump as he firmly guided
her through it, then pulled the door shut behind her, being
careful not to step in the pool of blood as he did so.

He was going to feel like a damned fool, he thought, if
he was wrong about her and she was gone when he got
back here with Marshal Durkee.

"A dead man?" There was an expression of disbelief on
the lawman's face as he sat behind his desk and looked up
at Boyd.

"How long have you been packing a badge, Marshal?"
Boyd asked innocently.

"Nigh on to forty years!"

"Then I reckon you've seen a few corpses in your time. Are you coming or not?"

"I'm comin', I'm comin'," Durkee grumbled as he pushed himself to his feet. He reached for his hat. "Now, where's this body you found?"

Boyd led him out of the office and down the street. On the way to the alley where the dead man lay, Boyd filled the marshal in on how he had come to discover the body.

"That gal you're talkin' about sounds like a whore called Rosie," Durkee commented. "I ain't never heard of her causin' any trouble. None of the old boys who visit her regular-like have come to me claimin' she robbed 'em or gave 'em a dose of the clap. You ask me, that's the kind of whore you need around a town."

Boyd didn't venture an opinion either way. He just took Durkee down the alley and around the back of the building, which was a run-down hotel that had seen much better days. The body was lying where Boyd had left it, evidently undisturbed.

Durkee grunted when he saw the corpse, and his leathery skin went a little pale under its lifelong tan. So much blood was bound to be a little shocking, even to a veteran lawman such as Durkee.

"Lonnie Colson," the marshal said. "That fits with what the gal told you."

"Who was he?" Boyd asked.

"I just told you. Oh, you mean what was he like? Well, he was pretty much a no-account. Not what I'd call a troublemaker, though. He did odd jobs around town, and he could cowboy all right when he put his mind to it. Signed on with some of the spreads around here whenever he needed money, but he never stuck with a job for long. Only times I had him in my jail was when he'd get a little drunk and get mixed up in a fight. Didn't happen very often."

"Who would want to do something like that to him?"

Durkee hunkered on his heels next to the dead man and made a quick search through his clothes. Colson was wearing a shirt with the buttons fastened wrong and a pair of denim pants. He had a pair of dirty socks on his feet, but no boots or shoes.

"Nothin' on him but the makin's," Durkee said after a moment. He started to straighten, then lifted a hand to Boyd. "Give me a hand here, son. These old bones don't unbend as easy as they used to."

Boyd grasped the marshal's wrist and helped him get to his feet. Durkee blew out his breath, arched his back to ease his spine a little, and went on. "Thanks, McMasters. Now, as I was sayin', there ain't no money on him. What's that suggest to you?"

"Robbery," Boyd said.

"Yep, me too. Let's talk to the gal."

Durkee stepped over to the door and knocked on it. "You in there, Rosie?" he called.

The door opened. The young blonde had brushed her hair, wiped some of the makeup off her face and straightened up the rest, and pulled on a simple cotton dress. She looked pale but composed, and Boyd noticed she carefully kept her gaze from falling on Lonnie Colson's body.

"What can I do for you, Marshal?" she asked.

"You can tell me the same thing you told this fella," Durkee said a little impatiently, jerking a thumb over his shoulder at Boyd. "What happened back here?"

"I . . . I wish I knew. Lonnie, well, paid for my time last night."

"Had money, did he?" Durkee asked quickly.

"Oh, sure. He had a whole poke full of coins."

Durkee glanced meaningfully at Boyd. "Yeah? Go on."

"Well . . . we both went to sleep, I guess. Lonnie'd paid for the rest of the night, you know, and for . . . for a girl like me who doesn't really start working again until late in the afternoon, that means I wouldn't have run him off for a while yet. I . . . I sort of remember somebody knocking on the door, and Lonnie got up to answer it. . . ." Rosie broke off her story and swallowed hard. It was a moment before she could go on. "I guess I dozed off again. Somebody yelled outside, and that woke me up. But then I didn't get up right away, because I didn't figure it was any of my business. I just stayed in bed until I heard this noise . . . this awful little gurgling noise . . ."

Which would have been Lonnie Colson breathing his last, Boyd figured.

"And then I got up and put my robe on, and I looked out, and . . . well, I was so scared when I saw him that I just went running away up the alley and out onto the street without paying any attention to where I was going. That's how come I ran into this . . . this gentleman here." She nodded toward Boyd.

He tugged on the brim of his hat and introduced himself. "Boyd McMasters, ma'am."

"Ain't no need for pleasantries," Durkee snapped. "Just like there ain't no doubt about what happened here. Lonnie Colson never was shy about lettin' folks know when he had some money in his pocket. I figure somebody heard about the stake he'd made and followed the two of you back here, Rosie. Then whoever it was waited until he was sure Lonnie would be good an' groggy before knockin' on the door, callin' him out, and cuttin' his throat. That how it looks to you, McMasters? You're the detective, after all."

Boyd bit back the angry retort that tried to spring to his lips. Durkee's attitude was annoying, but Boyd supposed he could understand it. When he had been the sheriff of Reeves County, he might well have resented any outsider who had come into his jurisdiction to conduct an investigation.

"Looks like it could have happened that way, all right," Boyd said. "I sure don't have any other explanation for it. But it's none of my business either."

"Nope," Durkee agreed. "You just reported it, that's all. You can go on your way now, McMasters. I'll get the undertaker down here to haul off poor Lonnie's carcass." He looked over at Rosie. "I'm plumb sorry about this, but it

could've been worse. At least you got paid before
somebody carved ol' Lonnie a new grin.''

That callous comment set Rosie to sobbing again, so
Boyd did what the marshal had suggested.

He got the hell out while the getting was good.

It was a good thing Natalie Clark had parted company with
him before the soiled dove called Rosie came running out
of that alley and bumped into him, Boyd reflected as he
rode west out of Silver Creek. He didn't know Natalie that
well yet, but he was sure she would have wanted to go with
him down that alley. If the sight of so much blood had
gotten to Rosie, hardened prostitute that she was, he could
only imagine what it might have done to a lady like Natalie.
She could have up and swooned, right then and there.

He pushed the incident out of his thoughts and mulled
over instead what he had accomplished so far today. It
didn't add up to much, as far as he could see. He had
learned more of the lay of the land, confronted Mike Torrance, and sent a telegram to his brother back in Oklahoma
City. There was no way of knowing which—if any—of
those maneuvers was going to pay off.

The simplest answer was usually the right answer, he had
learned, both in his time as a sheriff and his days as a field
agent for the CPA. Most lawbreakers lacked the ambition,
not to mention the intelligence, to put together complicated
schemes in order to carry out their villainy. Those bulls
were worth twenty thousand dollars, he recalled. Some
hardcases might have drifted into Silver Creek, heard about
the valuable bulls on Jonas Fletcher's ranch, and ridden out
there to steal them. Even the stupidest desperado could get
lucky sometimes. If that was what had happened, the
thieves would have driven the bulls to wherever they felt
was both close and yet far enough away to be safe, then
sold the animals. In that case, Boyd would have his work
cut out for him, because he would have to visit every livestock market in the northern half of Texas, asking questions

until he found somebody who remembered those bulls.

On the other hand, the way the thieves had covered their tracks and eluded pursuit seemed to indicate a good knowledge of the country hereabouts, something that drifting outlaws might not possess. But Mike Torrance would have known where that stretch of rocky ground was, Boyd was willing to bet. And Torrance was a long-standing enemy of Jonas Fletcher's. That theory hung together just as well as, if not better than, the other one.

Boyd sighed. He was going to have to pay another visit to the Rocking T, this one on the sly, and take a good long look around. Torrance's ranch was a big place, and he might have those bulls stashed somewhere on it.

If he ran into Mitch Riley or any of the other Torrance punchers, Boyd knew, there might not be anybody around to put a stop to any gunplay that broke out. He would be risking his life if he went wandering around the ranch.

But hell, that was why the Association paid him so much money, right?

That was the thought going through his head when something whistled past his ear and the grulla went down, hard.

Thirteen

Instinct took over as the horse fell. Boyd kicked his feet free from the stirrups and threw himself out of the saddle. He landed awkwardly, his shoulder striking painfully against the hard-packed dirt of the road, but that was better than having a dead horse land on his leg and pin him down.

Because the grulla was dead, there was no doubt about that. The slug that had narrowly missed Boyd's head had traveled on past to catch the horse in the neck, ripping a huge hole in the flesh and probably shattering the animal's spine. It hadn't even kicked any as it went down.

Another bullet slammed into the ground not far from Boyd's head, throwing dust into his eyes. This time he heard the heavy crack of the rifle, a sound he hadn't noticed the first time as he was more concerned with making sure the horse didn't fall on him. He scrambled to his feet and flung himself forward, vaulting over the grulla's body to land on the far side of the horse from the bushwhacker— or bushwhackers, since he wasn't sure just how many of the sons of bitches were shooting at him.

A bullet thudded into the horse's body. Boyd felt the impact through the dead flesh against which he was huddled.

Anger seethed inside him. He had halfway expected someone to try to ambush him, but now that it had actually happened, he was almost consumed with the need to strike back. He took a couple of deep breaths to calm himself down, grimacing at the coppery smell of the blood that had spilled from the grulla's wound. He had seen and smelled too much blood today.

Luck had been with him. The horse had fallen so that the saddle boot containing the big .70-caliber rifle was up where he could get it. Boyd waited until another shot had smacked into the grulla's body, then lifted himself and reached quickly for the stock of the rifle. His fingers closed around it and he yanked it from the saddle boot. A bullet whined past his head.

He fell onto his back, cradling the rifle on his chest. So far, he hadn't been able to pinpoint where the shots were coming from, only the general direction, which was off to the northeast. He tried to remember what he had passed during the couple of minutes before the first shot killed the grulla. There was a hogback ridge with some live oaks on top of it, he recalled. The ridge wasn't very high, but a man hiding on top of it in those trees would have a good view of the road. Good enough to pick off a rider moving along the trail.

Boyd took another deep breath, then raised up and thrust the barrel of the rifle over the body of the horse. The wooded ridge came into his sights and he squeezed the trigger. The .70-caliber kicked hard against his shoulder as the rifle blasted. He ducked behind the grulla again.

There! At least the bastard would know now that he still had some fangs.

Boyd's breath hissed between his teeth as the bush-whacker fired three times, fast. The bullets slammed into the grulla. The poor horse was getting shot to pieces, and sooner or later it might not stop all the slugs. Boyd could tell from the bushwhacker's reaction that his shot had come close enough to make the man angry.

He tried another one, popping up just long enough to sight in on the ridge and pull the trigger. As he ducked behind the horse's body again, he spotted something out of the corner of his eye.

Down the road, back toward Silver Creek, a small plume of dust was rising into the air.

Somebody was coming, Boyd realized. Until now, he had been alone on the road, which was a perfect setup for the ambush attempt. But if the would-be killer was going to keep firing, he would soon have to deal with at least one witness.

That might prove to be pretty dangerous to the witness, Boyd realized grimly. He didn't want anybody else's death on his conscience. When the traveler came closer, Boyd might have to try to warn him—or them—somehow.

Unless he could drive off the bushwhacker first.

This time it was his turn to fire as fast as he could. He came up in a crouch and threw four shots at the top of the ridge, squeezing them off as quickly as he could work the lever of the rifle in between. Those heavy slugs with the carpet tacks pushed into their noses had to be tearing big holes through the brush up there. Even at this distance, Boyd saw tree branches leap into the air as he peppered the woods.

He was rewarded with a sudden glimpse of someone moving rapidly through the oaks. Boyd tried to sight in on the figure and fired a couple more times, but the bushwhacker kept moving. Whoever it was, he was too far away for Boyd to make out any details in the brief moment before he veered off and disappeared behind the ridge.

Boyd hunkered down again behind the horse, just in case there were two of them and they were trying to trick him. But as time stretched out and no more shots came searching for him, he decided that the bushwhacker had indeed fled. Boyd glanced down the road, saw that the dust had stopped. He could make out a wagon that was no longer moving. Whoever was driving had heard the shots and had the sense not to come any closer.

Boyd stood up, lifted the rifle in both hands above his

head for a moment, then bent over and placed the weapon beside the body of the horse. He stepped away from the animal, holding his now-empty hands well clear of him. After a few seconds, the wagon started forward again.

When it drew close enough for him to make out some details, Boyd saw that a man and a woman were on the seat, the woman handling the reins of the mule team that pulled the wagon while the man hefted a shotgun with long twin barrels. Boyd didn't make any sudden moves, and put a smile on his face as the wagon approached.

"Howdy, folks," he called when the man and woman were in earshot. "I could sure use a helping hand."

The woman hauled back on the reins, bringing the mules to a stop. The man held the shotgun so that its barrels were pointing in Boyd's general direction as he asked, "What happened here, mister?"

Boyd thought now that he recognized the couple. This was one of the wagons he had passed on his way into Silver Creek earlier in the day. The vehicle had been loaded with produce then, and now it was empty. It had been a good day at the market for these farmers.

With a nod toward the grulla, Boyd said, "I was ambushed. Somebody shot my horse right out from under me and then tried to do for me too. Might have if you folks hadn't come along and spooked him."

The man grunted. "More'n likely it was you shootin' back at him with that damned big rifle there. Libbie and I heard the shots. Sounded almost like you were firin' a cannon."

Boyd grinned a little. "It does pack a wallop," he admitted. "My name's Boyd McMasters. I'm working for Jonas Fletcher."

The woman said, "You're the range detective who's looking for those bulls somebody stole from Mr. Fletcher, aren't you?"

"Yes, ma'am, I reckon I am." Boyd tried not to show his surprise. It looked like everybody in Silver Creek and the surrounding area knew who he was now. Word traveled mighty fast in these parts. "If you folks could see your way clear to taking me back to the JF Connected, I'd be obliged. It's still several miles, and that's a long walk in riding boots."

"It sure is," the man said. He finally lowered the barrels of the shotgun so that they pointed toward the floorboard of the wagon. "Climb up in back," he offered, jerking a thumb over his shoulder. "Plenty of room, and it ain't too far out of our way to go by Fletcher's place, I reckon."

"Thanks. Like I said, I'm obliged." Boyd bent over and picked up his hat, which had gone flying off his head when he jumped clear of the grulla. He slapped it against his leg to get some of the dust off it, then settled it on his head. He gathered up his rifle and put it in the back of the wagon, then with the man's help got the saddle off the grulla and tossed it in too, before stepping up into the wagon bed himself.

The farmer's name was Vince Randolph, and his wife was Libbie. They were friendly enough once they decided that Boyd wasn't going to start shooting at them, especially Libbie, who was full of questions about the missing bulls. Since Jonas Fletcher and Mike Torrance were the wealthiest, most influential citizens of the county, naturally most people were interested in this latest ruckus between them. And the fact that someone had just tried to bushwhack Boyd made him even more interesting. Though he was grateful to the Randolphs for their assistance, Boyd was still glad when the wagon reached the Fletcher ranch house and he could bid them farewell with his thanks.

Jonas Fletcher emerged from the house as Boyd dropped his saddle on the porch. "What in blazes happened?" Fletcher asked. "Where's your horse, McMasters?"

"On the road about halfway between Silver Creek and the turnoff for your place," Boyd replied. "Dead."

"Dead!"

"Somebody tried to put a rifle slug through my head. It

missed me but got the grulla instead. Whoever it was took a few more potshots at me, but I guess I put up more of a fight than the bushwhacker expected. He rode off in a hurry, and then a farm wagon came along and picked me up, brought me back here.''

"Who'd want to ambush you like that?"

"I can answer that," Chuck Fletcher said as he came around the corner of the house in time to hear the last of Boyd's story and his brother's question. "It was Mike Torrance, wasn't it, Boyd?"

Boyd shrugged. "I never got a good enough look at the son of a buck to tell for sure. But it could have been Torrance."

"By God, he's gone too far this time!" Fletcher exclaimed. "I've got a good mind to gather the men and ride up there. We'll teach Torrance a lesson he won't soon forget!"

From the doorway of the house came another voice. Belinda cried, "No, Daddy!"

Fletcher swung toward her, his face angry. "What are you afraid of? That your precious Griff might get himself shot? Well, it'd be good riddance as far as I'm concerned."

Even through the screen door, Boyd could tell how pale and tightly drawn Belinda's face was. But there was something more than fear in her features. There was outrage too.

"I'm starting to understand why Mother left," she said in a low voice. "I've been confused all these years about why she would do such a thing, but now I think I know."

Fletcher took a step toward the door. He said, "You hush up, Belinda. I don't want you talking about your mother."

"Why not? Are you afraid I'm going to turn out to be just like her?"

"Shut up!" Fletcher's voice rose. "I won't have you talking like that!"

Chuck stepped up onto the porch and went to his brother's side. As he put a hand on Fletcher's shoulder, he said, "Now, Jonas, you shouldn't get mad at Belinda."

Roughly, Fletcher shrugged off Chuck's hand. "Why the hell not?"

As Boyd watched intently, Chuck seemed to gather his courage. It was only rarely, if ever, Boyd thought, that the younger brother stood up to the older one like this.

"It's not Belinda's fault," Chuck said stubbornly. "And besides, some of the men are watching, and this looks bad, Jonas, it looks damned bad."

Fletcher snorted in contempt. "What would a coward and a fool like you know about looking bad?" he demanded.

Chuck winced under the lash of his brother's harsh words, but he managed to say, "I've had a lot of experience at it. I know, Jonas. Believe me, I know."

Fletcher glanced at the bunkhouse and the barns, as did Boyd. Several of the JF Connected punchers were indeed standing around, well within earshot, and even if they were carefully looking the other way at the moment, it was obvious they had witnessed the confrontation between Fletcher and Belinda. Boyd took a step closer to the porch.

"Listen," he said sharply, "I was the one who got ambushed. That grulla was a good horse, but not so good that I want you starting a shooting war over him, Fletcher. Let's all calm down."

"I don't want to calm down," Belinda said raggedly. "I'm tired of calming down!"

She turned and vanished inside the house.

"Damn it!" Fletcher bit off. He looked at Boyd. "You're getting in the habit of talking to me like you run this place, McMasters, instead of me. I don't like it. I won't stand for it from Chuck, and I won't stand for it from you."

"Then you may have to find your own damned bulls," Boyd snapped. He spun on his heel and stalked toward the barns and the corrals. The least Fletcher could do was replace that grulla with a saddle mount from his own remuda.

He had only taken a few steps when he heard Fletcher

sigh and then say, "McMasters . . . wait a minute."

Boyd stopped and looked back over his shoulder. "Why?"

"So you can hear me say something I don't often say. I'm sorry." Fletcher came down the steps from the porch, followed by Chuck. "There. Are you satisfied? You're right, and I'm wrong."

"What about Belinda?"

Fletcher's tanned features hardened again. "Your job doesn't give you the right to interfere between a parent and a child."

"Point taken," Boyd said with a shrug. "But I'd take what that girl says seriously. Otherwise you may wake up and find her gone one of these days."

"She'll be gone sooner or later anyway," Fletcher said, with the bleak acceptance of all parents who know that eventually children grow up and leave home. He waved that off and continued. "I guess it wouldn't do any good to ride in shooting up at the Rocking T. It wouldn't get those bulls back. I'm just a mite tired from trying to be optimistic all the time in front of those buyers."

"Where are they, anyway?" Boyd asked. He hadn't seen any of the men who had come here to pick up the bulls.

"Mrs. Sumner and Miss Clark are lying down inside," Fletcher said. "Natalie said she saw you in town earlier."

"That's right," Boyd admitted. "We had lunch together, in fact."

"Natalie's a fine lady. You're a lucky man."

Boyd nodded and asked, "What about the others?"

"I sent them out with some of my hands for a tour of the ranch. Even Pat and Harry and Sarey Beth haven't seen all of the place, and they're old friends. Albie Clark complained that I was just trying to distract them . . . and I reckon he's right, whether I like it or not. *Did* you find out anything today?"

"Not for certain," Boyd said, knowing how frustrated Fletcher would be with that answer. Hell, he was pretty frustrated himself. All he really had to show for his day's work was a dead horse and a sore shoulder. "If you'll loan me another mount, I'll keep nosing around tomorrow."

"Take any of the horses you want from the corrals. You won't find a finer remuda in this part of Texas."

Boyd could believe that. Jonas Fletcher seemed to be running a first-class operation. The numerous cattle he had seen appeared to be sleek and fat, and the horses were as good as the rancher claimed. The buildings were all in good repair. Boyd had seen some run-down spreads in his time, but the JF Connected definitely didn't fall into that category.

It took money to keep such a place going, however, and once again Boyd wondered just what sort of financial shape Fletcher was really in. Maybe Warren's reply to the telegram he had sent would supply some answers.

"It's getting too late in the afternoon to do anything else today," Boyd said. "I'll get a fresh start in the morning."

Fletcher nodded. "That's fine." He glanced toward the house. "Speaking of fresh starts, I suppose I'd better go find Belinda. When she starts sulking, there's no telling what she'll do."

He went inside, leaving Chuck to stroll alongside Boyd as the field agent went to look over the saddle horses kept in one of the corrals. After a moment, Chuck said, "It *was* Torrance who took those shots at you, wasn't it?"

"Maybe. Don't forget, though, that fella Riley has a pretty good grudge against me too. He could have slipped off from the Rocking T and waited for me to come along the road from town."

"How would he have known you even went to Silver Creek?"

Boyd frowned. Chuck had asked a good question. Boyd had to shake his head and say, "I don't know. I hadn't thought of that."

"See, you need me to help you, Boyd. I knew all along I had the makings of a good detective."

Boyd gave a short, humorless laugh. "If you want to be a detective, maybe you can find out who cut Lonnie Colson's throat."

Chuck stopped short, grabbed Boyd's arm with surprising strength. "What did you say?" he demanded.

Boyd's frown deepened as he stopped and looked over at Chuck. The young man's eyes were wide, and his face was ashen.

All in all, Boyd thought, Chuck Fletcher looked like somebody was square dancing right over his grave.

Fourteen

Boyd looked down pointedly at Chuck's hand gripping his arm, and after a couple of seconds Chuck released him with a muttered apology. Boyd said, "You wouldn't know about it since it just happened this afternoon, but somebody killed a man named Lonnie Colson in Silver Creek. What's that to you, Chuck?"

"It just took me by surprise, that's all," Chuck said. "Lonnie was a friend of mine. Well, not a friend, really. We got drunk together a few times. That was all. What the hell happened to him?"

"He was with a whore named Rosie—"

"Rosie wouldn't have hurt Lonnie! She liked him."

"I didn't say she did," Boyd went on, trying to curb his impatience. "They were both asleep, and somebody knocked on the door of Rosie's room. Colson went to see who it was and got lured out into the back alley. Whoever it was sliced his throat open."

A shudder went through Chuck. "Lord, what a horrible way to die."

"There aren't very many good ways," Boyd said dryly.

"No, I suppose not. Poor ol' Lonnie."

"According to the girl, he had quite a bit of money. Quite a bit for him, anyway. Marshal Durkee figures that was why he was killed."

Chuck nodded slowly. "Lonnie did like to let everybody

know anytime he had more than two coins to rub together. I guess that habit finally caught up to him.'' He looked intently at Boyd. ''The marshal doesn't have any idea who did it?''

Boyd shook his head. ''Not that I could tell. Maybe he'll be able to turn up something . . . I wouldn't count on it.''

''I'm not,'' Chuck said, almost as much to himself as to Boyd.

''Come on. I've got to pick out a horse to replace that grulla.''

After a few minutes of studying the horses in the remuda, Boyd settled on a leggy chestnut gelding with a white blaze on his face. The horse appeared to be both intelligent and fast, a good combination. Maybe not the best one in the bunch for endurance, but Boyd didn't expect to have to make any long rides in the near future.

Chuck's reaction to the news of Lonnie Colson's murder still bothered him a little, but he supposed it was reasonable enough. Chuck was a young man, and this country wasn't as wild as it had once been, some fifteen or twenty years earlier. A man wasn't at constant risk from ruthless outlaws or marauding Indians anymore. Probably, Chuck just wasn't used to having his friends die, let alone be murdered so brutally. Colson's death was an all-too-grisly reminder to Chuck of his own mortality, Boyd figured. And that was enough to shake up most folks.

Boyd's own mortality didn't bother him a damned bit. Most of what was good and important in him had died along with Hannah, he figured, and what hadn't been destroyed then had perished in the violent aftermath of her death and the long drunken slide into near-oblivion. Now he was just a husk of a man.

But a husk of a man with a job still to do, he reminded himself.

The buyers returned from their tour of the ranch a little later. Enos Sumner and Albie Clark were both sullen, Clark even more than usual because his horse had come up lame and he'd had to wait under a tree while the others rode on, picking him up on the way back to the ranch house. He complained loudly about it, just as he complained about almost everything, as far as Boyd could see. Pat Sturdivant and the Olivers seemed to be growing more impatient. So far none of them had anything to show for the 2500 dollars they had each invested, and that situation was enough to make anyone edgy, even if they were friends with Jonas Fletcher.

The atmosphere at dinner that evening was subdued. Once again, Belinda refused to come to the table, so one of the Mexican women carried a tray up to her room. The conversation around the big table was sporadic at best, and the only person who seemed to be in a good mood was Natalie Clark. Her shopping trip to Silver Creek earlier in the day, followed by a nap, had refreshed and invigorated her.

"Well, this has been a good trip even if we don't get that bull," she said, ignoring the increasing pall that her words sent over the gathering. "I've certainly enjoyed it. I'm sorry I didn't get to take that tour of the ranch today, though."

Fletcher managed to summon up a weak smile. "I'm sure I could arrange for you to be shown around by yourself, Natalie. Or perhaps Mrs. Sumner would like to go along too."

Annabelle Sumner shuddered. "No, I don't believe so. Thank you anyway, Mr. Fletcher. I'm afraid I'm just not . . . not an outdoor girl."

That was putting it mildly, Boyd thought. More like a hothouse flower that wilted when it was exposed to the real world. But he kept it to himself, since there was no point in being rude.

"We can go for a ride tomorrow," Fletcher said to Natalie. "I'll show you the place myself."

"That's very kind of you, Jonas," she said with a smile.

Her brother spoke up, saying sourly, "I was hoping we'd

get those damned bulls tomorrow. But McMasters here doesn't seem to be any closer to finding them. Are you McMasters?''

"I've got a lead or two to follow up," Boyd said, unwilling to admit his lack of progress to Clark.

"Oh? And what would they be? Tell us."

Boyd didn't like the smug little smile of disbelief on Clark's face, and he might have responded angrily if Chuck hadn't jumped in to say, "A good detective never shares his theories until he has proof. Isn't that right, Boyd?"

"Right enough," Boyd said with a curt nod.

"You know," Chuck continued, "I was reading this magazine I got in Fort Worth a while back, and it had this story about an English fella named Holmes, and he was quite a detective, yes, sir. All he had to do was shake hands with a gent he'd never met before, and then this Mr. Holmes could tell you just about everything there was to know about the man, like where he came from and what he did for a living and, shoot, even what kind of dog he had at home. It was something, I tell you."

"All that stuff is just made up," Sumner said harshly. "It doesn't have anything to do with real life."

The comment made everyone fall silent again, and Chuck looked rather abashed.

But maybe Chuck had something there, Boyd mused. It was easy for a storybook detective to figure everything out, since coming along behind him was always some writer who could make everything turn out all right in the end anyway. In real life things weren't always so neat. But keeping your eyes and ears open was the key, both in fiction and reality, Boyd thought. He found his brain going back over everything he had seen and heard since his arrival in Silver Creek, twisting it this way and that, finding new ways to look at it all. For an instant he thought he could make out the first glimmerings of a picture, but it was just a distant glimpse through fog. . . .

And then, as Natalie Clark stood up and went behind his

chair on her way out of the dining room and brushed his shoulder with her hip, it was gone. Whatever it had been.

"I'm sorry," she murmured, laying a hand on his shoulder for a second.

Boyd looked up at her and smiled. "Don't be," he told her.

That night, after he had blown out the lamp in his room, he stretched out on the bed wearing the bottoms of his summer-weight long underwear and stared up at the darkened ceiling. Once again, he began trying to remember everything that had occurred since he had begun his investigation, in hopes of recapturing the elusive image that had almost come to him earlier. Now, though, the pieces of his memory wouldn't come together in anything that even resembled good sense. Boyd let out a long sigh.

And then a floorboard creaked right outside the door of his room.

Instinct sent his hand to the butt of his holstered revolver, which was hanging on the headboard near his pillow. As his fingers closed around the grips, he heard the doorknob rattle slightly as it began to turn. Nobody in the house had any reason to wish him harm—as far as he knew—but he wasn't in the habit of taking chances either. Steel whispered against leather as he slid the gun from its holster.

He had the gun leveled at the door as it opened. Faint light from somewhere down the hall silhouetted the person standing there. Boyd saw a slender yet curved figure with honey-blond hair tumbling around her shoulders, and he relaxed slightly. Not completely, though. He lowered the gun but still held it ready.

"Sneaking around like that's a good way to get yourself shot," he said.

Natalie Clark gasped. "Oh, dear!" she said. "I thought you'd be asleep by now."

"I've got a lot on my mind," Boyd said.

"So do I." Natalie came into the room and shut the door

softly behind her, cutting off the light. Now she was just a pale shape in the darkness as she came toward the bed. "I've been thinking about a great many things, Boyd."

He reached out with his free hand and found one of the matches that had been left on the bedside table beside the oil lamp. The flick of a thumbnail sent flame spurting from the head of the match. Natalie stepped back, squinting against the sudden glare, but Boyd had his eyes narrowed and was ready for it.

He hadn't really been worried about her slipping into his room with a gun or a knife, but even if he had been, that concern would have been alleviated. There was no place to hide a weapon in the gauzy nightdress she wore. It floated around her, seeming almost weightless, and her smooth creamy skin was visible through it. Dark brown nipples showed plainly against the thin material, and so did the triangle of hair at the juncture of her thighs. She was undeniably beautiful.

Her eyes were adjusting to the light too, because she said, "Oh, my goodness, Boyd, you don't need that gun. Did you think I was trying to hurt you?"

"I didn't know who was sneaking in here," he explained as he slid the gun back into its holster. "After being bushwhacked earlier today . . ."

"I understand," Natalie said as she came closer to the bed. "That must have been terrible. I know you didn't say much about it at supper. . . . "

"It goes with the job," he said, not really wanting to discuss it now either. He felt a hardening at his groin that had a mind of its own. He leaned over, lit the lamp, and shook the match out.

Natalie moved to the edge of the bed and sat down without being invited. Maybe she took the lump in his underwear as invitation enough, Boyd thought. He smelled the clean fragrance of her and wanted to reach out and touch her. Before he gave in to that urge, however, he had to be sure she was here only for what seemed to be the obvious reason.

"You said there were things on your mind," he prodded.

She nodded solemnly. "I'm afraid Albie's going to lose what little patience he has left and demand his money back from Jonas. When that happens, we'll be leaving and going back to Waco."

Boyd nodded. "I imagine so."

"But I don't want to go home yet!" she protested. "Like I said at dinner, I've enjoyed this trip, and I don't want to go back. I'm going to try to talk Albie into giving Jonas some more time, but I don't think he'll listen to me. Not unless I can tell him you're sure that you'll find those bulls soon."

"I can't promise that," Boyd said after a second's hesitation. "I'll track them down eventually, I'm confident of that, but I don't know how long it'll take."

Natalie sighed and leaned closer to him. "Well, then, I guess I'm just going to have to make the most of the time I have left. The time *we* have left . . ."

Her lips met his.

Boyd didn't pull away from the kiss. For a moment, he didn't return it either, as images of both Hannah and Martha floated through his mind. It was bad enough he kept being disloyal to Hannah's memory with Martha, but now he wanted Natalie Clark too. What kind of man was he? he asked himself.

Just a man, he decided, a man who had been wounded emotionally, who had come back from the brink of nothingness, who was learning that the appetites of a human being were the most stubborn things on earth.

Just a man who wanted to make love to this woman . . .

His arms went around her and his tongue thrust into her mouth, savoring the wet heat of her. She clutched at him, one hand moving through the mat of hair on his chest while the other slid down his stomach and abdomen to caress the

hard length of his shaft through his underwear. After a moment she tugged at the buttons, loosening them, and freed
him from the tight confines of the garment. His hips lifted
involuntarily as her warm fingers closed around the pole of
urgent flesh.

Boyd's fingers found a tie at the neck of her gown and
pulled it loose. He spread it open so that he could cup her
breasts, kneading the creamy globes as he played his
thumbs across the pebbled nipples.

Natalie was gasping for breath as she broke the kiss. She
threw her head back as Boyd lifted first one breast, then
the other, and drew the nipples between his lips. He sucked
hard on them, then opened his mouth wider to engulf as
much of each soft mound as he could. Natalie's hand
pumped on his organ, squeezing tightly as her fingers slid
up and down on the shaft. After a moment Boyd had to
catch her wrist and disengage her grip to keep her from
bringing him to a climax too soon.

She let out a little moan of disappointment, but it
changed to a gurgle of pleasure as he rolled her onto her
back, parted her thighs, and plunged his head between
them. He kissed his way through the silky, fine-spun hair,
his own excitement growing as her musk filled his nostrils.
Then he found the wet core of her with his lips and tongue.
Her fingers twined in his hair and held him there as her
hips began to thrust against him. With each movement, his
tongue plunged into her. In moments she was bucking
wildly, and Boyd had the sudden hope that she wasn't a
screamer. That could prove to be downright embarrassing.

She wasn't. Her culmination came in a series of breaths
that hissed through her clenched teeth. Her back arched off
the bed for a long moment as her juices flooded and ecstasy
raced along every nerve in her body; then she sagged, completely spent. Boyd kissed her stomach and then each breast
again as she lay with eyes closed, murmuring dreamily.

Her lassitude lasted only a moment. Then she lifted herself, pushed down on his shoulders, and whispered, "Now it's your turn."

Boyd stretched out on the bed and let her finish pulling the long underwear off his legs. Then she knelt between his knees, caressing him with one hand while the other cupped his sac for a moment before she bent over and took him in her mouth.

The feel of her warm lips closing around him was almost enough to make him explode then and there, but he held off somehow, aided by the tight grip of her fingers around the base of his stalk as she licked and sucked on it. Long, maddening moments passed. She brought him to the edge more than once, only to back away. His entire body was quivering, every nerve alive and throbbing. Finally, when he couldn't stand it any longer, he reached down, caught her shoulders, and pulled her up on top of him. She reached for him to guide him into her, but even before her fingers found his shaft the tip of it had lodged against her soaked opening and surged into it. She let out another gasp.

Natalie sat up straight so that he sank deeper and ever deeper into her, until he had probed her depths as far as he could go. She began to pump her hips back and forth as she clutched at his chest. Her eyes closed and she whispered, "Oh, my God, yes, yes, yes . . ."

She rode him that way for several minutes, Boyd keeping his hips relatively still, but then neither of them could stand to wait any longer. He began to thrust up to meet her. Her breasts bobbed madly until he reached up and grabbed them, his fingers sinking into the soft flesh. Natalie moaned, completely in the grip of passion. Boyd felt his climax approaching, washing through him like waves. He moved his hands to her hips, holding her to him as he drove into her.

Then he was erupting, long, incredible tremors that drained him, his juices filling her and mingling with her own. A flush spread over Natalie's chest above her breasts, and he heard those same hissing breaths that marked her fulfillment. His shaft was still pumping and spurting, and it gave a last couple of jets as she fell forward onto his chest, gasping for breath.

After a moment, she lifted her head and looked at him. "Lord, what a bull you are, Boyd McMasters!"

He laughed, and ran his hand down the smooth lines of her back to the curve of her buttocks. "I'll take that as a compliment," he said.

"Oh, it was. It was!"

She rested her head on his shoulder. Boyd hoped she wouldn't go to sleep there. As much as he had enjoyed this interlude, her last comment had reminded him of why he was here in Texas in the first place.

There were still those missing bulls to find—as well as a mysterious bushwhacker.

And who could guess what new trouble the morning would bring?

Fifteen

"I've had enough!" Albie Clark said angrily. "I'm tired of your stalling, Fletcher. The bull I paid twenty-five hundred for is gone, and you don't have any idea when you'll get him back—if ever! I want my money. I'm going home."

The outburst came at the breakfast table the next morning as everyone sat around trying to ignore the gloomy atmosphere that gripped the place. Clark was not going to allow the problem to go ignored any longer, however, and he shook off his sister's hand as Natalie tried to intercede.

"Now, Albie," Jonas Fletcher began, a hint of desperation in his voice, "you know that McMasters here is going to find those bulls—"

"I don't know any such thing," Clark cut in. "Even though he won't admit it, I know damn well he hasn't made a bit of progress."

Boyd lifted his coffee cup, sipped the strong black brew, and didn't say anything. He wasn't going to waste his breath defending himself to a jackass like Clark.

"That's not fair," Fletcher said. "McMasters has only had one full day to work on the case. Hell, nobody could find those bulls in that amount of time, no matter how good a detective he was!"

Clark snorted in disgust. "You can talk all you want, but the simple fact of the matter is this: I paid you that money in good faith. Now that you can't deliver the bull and keep your part of the bargain, I want my money back. The law's going to be on my side in this, Fletcher. Don't make me fetch the sheriff out here.''

Pat Sturdivant said, ''Here now! You got no call to go talkin' about bringin' in the law, Mr. Clark. Jonas Fletcher is an honorable man, and a reasonable cuss too.'' The elderly rancher looked at Fletcher. ''What about it, Jonas? You ain't tryin' to swindle nobody, are you?''

''Of course not,'' Fletcher replied impatiently. ''I've told all of you the truth—''

''After we made the trip up here,'' Clark declared. ''You knew those bulls were gone. You should have gotten in touch with us and saved us the trip. Hell, you could have sent bank drafts to all of us and settled the whole thing. Then, when you recover the bulls—if you ever do—you could have gotten in touch with us again. Chances are we'd have still bought what you were selling.''

Albie Clark was a thoroughly unpleasant man, Boyd thought—but in this case, Clark was right. Once the bulls were stolen, Fletcher should have proceeded in just the manner Clark had outlined.

Unless, Boyd suddenly realized, there was some reason he couldn't.

That thought would do with some mulling over, Boyd decided. In the meantime, something had to be done about Clark's demand for his money back.

''Listen, Clark,'' Boyd said sharply, cutting through the hubbub around the table. ''I'm going to find those bulls— and soon.''

Clark blinked owlishly and frowned at him. ''You are?''

''That's right. I'm closer than I've let on,'' Boyd lied.

He couldn't have said where the words came from. Maybe it was just that he disliked Clark enough to want to get the man's goat. Maybe it was loyalty to the man whose trouble had brought him here.

Or maybe he was just hungry for Natalie and wanted a

chance for a repeat of the previous night's lovemaking before Clark went storming back to Waco and took his sister with him.

"See, I told you," Fletcher said triumphantly, although he shot a glance toward Boyd that said more clearly than words, *God, I hope you're telling the truth!* "I have complete faith in McMasters' ability."

Sarey Beth Oliver said, "Nobody asked my opinion, but I reckon we ought to give Jonas and Mr. McMasters some more time. Shoot, one day's not long enough to find anything!"

"I agree," Sturdivant put in. "We ought to wait at least a week—"

"A week!" Enos Sumner exclaimed, beating Clark to the punch. "Coming up here has already cost me almost a week. I don't have another one to waste."

"Four days!" Fletcher said. "How about that?" He looked at Boyd. "That should be long enough for you to finish the job, shouldn't it?"

Boyd frowned, wishing that Fletcher hadn't pinned him down to such a tight schedule. But he nodded anyway, since he had already started lying, and said, "Four days should be plenty."

"It's settled then," Fletcher continued quickly, not giving Clark or Sumner a chance to haggle any more. "You'll have those bulls in four days or less."

Boyd glanced down the table at Chuck Fletcher, who hadn't taken part in the argument. Chuck didn't look happy, and he was a far cry from the seemingly happy-go-lucky young prankster he had been when Boyd first met him a couple of days earlier. Folks could change in a hurry, though . . . and maybe Chuck hadn't really been as happy-go-lucky to start with as he had appeared to be.

Belinda wasn't happy these days, that was for sure. Boyd had caught a glimpse of her earlier in the upstairs hall. She was red-faced and hollow-eyed, not nearly as seductive as when he had first met her, and she had turned away from him quickly. Obviously, she was still upset and crying a lot. She hadn't come downstairs for a meal since he had been there on the JF Connected. If he hadn't known better, he might have thought she was just trying to avoid him.

He wouldn't be wanting for female companionship, though, not as long as Natalie was around. They had made love for a second time the previous night, before she slipped out of his room and went back to her own. She wasn't treating him any differently this morning, however, and he was glad of that. The last thing he needed right now was for her to make it obvious they had become lovers. That would only complicate matters.

Still, at the same time he was looking forward to the night again, and another chance to sate himself with her smooth, creamy, sweetly driven body.

In the meantime, there was work to do. Boyd pushed his chair back and stood up. "I'm riding into Silver Creek again this morning," he said, "but before I go I want to talk to you in private, Mr. Fletcher."

The rancher frowned. "I promised to show Miss Clark around the spread today."

"This won't take long," Boyd said.

"Oh, go ahead, Jonas," Natalie told him. "I don't mind waiting a little while."

"All right. If you're sure." Fletcher stood up and faced Boyd. "Let's go into my office."

Fletcher led the way to the room. Boyd glanced behind them to make sure no one was following them, then shut the door. Fletcher went behind the desk but didn't sit down. He didn't offer Boyd a chair either.

"What is it?" he asked rather curtly.

Boyd smiled thinly. "You sound a mite impatient for somebody who just had his bacon pulled out of the fire. If you'd had to give Clark his money back, Sumner would have wanted his too. Maybe even Sturdivant and the Olivers would have wanted theirs."

Fletcher shook his head. "They're my friends."

"And you're damned lucky to have them too."

Fletcher sighed wearily, lifted a hand to rub at his temples. "I know it, and I'm sorry I sounded abrupt when we came in here. That was damned close to a disaster out there this morning."

"Why?"

Fletcher lifted his head and frowned at the simple question. "Why what?"

"Why would it have been a disaster?"

"You mean, to give back all that money?"

"You've got the money, don't you?" Boyd said.

Fletcher's jaw tightened until a little muscle jumped in his cheek, but he didn't say anything.

"By God, that's it," Boyd said quietly. "You don't *have* their money anymore."

"I told you, a place like this takes cash to operate," Fletcher snapped. "Did you ever run a ranch, McMasters?"

Boyd's mind went back for a second to West Texas, to the small spread and the neat, whitewashed house outside of Pecos. His spread . . . his house . . . his and Hannah's.

"I ran a ranch," he said, his voice as hard as stone.

"Then you know how sometimes you can get strapped for cash, even when everything is going all right. I . . . had some problems. Financial reverses, the robber barons back East call it when it happens to them. I had to have that money to pay on a note at the bank in Silver Creek."

Boyd might have been able to get some of this information from his brother Warren, through the Cattleman's Association, but he preferred hearing it straight from Fletcher. He had sensed it was time to clear the air, which was why he had wanted this discussion with the rancher in the first place.

"I thought this ranch belonged to you and your brother free and clear," Boyd said. "I thought you inherited it."

"We did. But it was nothing then, not much more than a hardscrabble farm. *I* was the one who built it into the largest ranch in North Texas."

"And you borrowed a lot of money along the way."

Fletcher shrugged his shoulders. "You know the old saying. It takes money to make money."

Boyd sighed. These revelations put things in a somewhat different light, without altering the basic problem of the stolen bulls. Now he understood Fletcher's desperation . . . or some of it, anyway, as he realized a moment later as Fletcher went on.

"It's actually worse than what it looks like," Fletcher said. "The payment those buyers made just paid off part of the note. The rest of it is going to come due in less than a month. The bank's given me all the time it's going to."

"So unless you get those bulls back, and collect the other ten thousand—"

"I'll lose the ranch, more than likely," Fletcher said, his voice grim but quiet and restrained.

"You mean you and Chuck will lose the ranch," Boyd pointed out.

Fletcher shrugged. "Legally, I suppose you're right, but I've never thought of Chuck as half-owner of the ranch. I know he hasn't either." He gave a short, humorless bark of laughter. "Chuck wouldn't want that much responsibility."

"Does he know how desperate your money problem is?"

"I just told you—he wouldn't *want* to know."

"He's got a right," Boyd said. "The place is half his."

Fletcher's eyes narrowed. "There you go again, talking to me like that. One of these days, I might just take a swing at you, McMasters."

Boyd met the other man's hostile gaze squarely. "Whenever you're ready," he said. "But in the meantime, I was sent down here to do a job, and I mean to do it."

"Go ahead. Nobody's stopping you."

Boyd nodded and turned to leave the office. Nothing said you had to like the man you were working for, he thought, and at this moment, he didn't like Jonas Fletcher much at all. The man was capable of being a genuine asshole, in fact.

Chuck was waiting near the office door but not right outside. "What are you going to do now, Boyd?" he asked eagerly. "Was that true about you having some leads?"

"Like I said, I'm riding into Silver Creek," Boyd replied. "I want to check on a few things."

"Well, can I come with you?"

"I think you'd better stay here, Chuck, and sort of keep an eye on things for me."

Chuck's eyes widened. "You'd trust me to do that?"

"Sure." That would keep him occupied, Boyd thought. "I want you to watch Clark and Sumner especially."

Chuck nodded. "I'll do it. I'll sure do it, Boyd."

"I knew I could count on you." Boyd turned away, went on to the front door, and snagged his hat from one of the pegs on the wall near the door. He went out and headed for the corrals, circling the house as he did so.

He didn't feel guilty for giving Chuck a meaningless chore to do. He hadn't forgotten that ambush attempt the day before. From the looks of things, it was going to be dangerous for anybody who was too close to him until he found out exactly what was going on around here. He was hoping the visit to Silver Creek this morning might clear up a few questions.

Warren had had plenty of time now to respond to his telegram. Boyd didn't know why no one had brought the reply out to the ranch, but he intended to find out. He would pay a visit to Morrison's Drug Store, where the telegraph office was located, then maybe stop by the marshal's office too. Since he had been involved with the discovery of Lonnie Colson's body, he was naturally curious to know if Marshal Durkee had found out anything about the man's murder.

Boyd took care of saddling the blaze-faced chestnut himself, even though one of the ranch hands offered to do it for him. A man rode better when he had tightened his own

cinches, Boyd believed. Without saying good-bye to anyone, he pointed the horse north on the trail that led to the
main road.

It was another pretty morning, blue sky and white clouds
and the warmth of the sun already growing. Boyd followed
the trail through the oak-dotted landscape, his eyes con-
stantly moving as he studied his surroundings. He didn't
expect anybody would try to bushwhack him while he was
still on Fletcher's range, but any suspicious movement, any
flash of sunlight off metal, would warn him that something
might be about to happen.

Nothing did. He reached the road without seeing anybody except some cows and the JF Connected hands who
were moving them from one pasture to another. After a
quick look around at the place where the trail intersected
the main road—it was damned hard to shake the feeling
that he was being watched somehow—he turned the chestnut's head east toward Silver Creek.

A half hour passed with no sign of trouble, and he knew
he ought to be getting close to the settlement. It wasn't
quite within sight yet, however, when he spotted another
rider coming toward him. There was only one man on
horseback, and he didn't seem threatening. Boyd moved the
chestnut over a little to give the other rider plenty of room.

The pilgrim reined in, however, and Boyd saw that he
was a young man, a boy really, not yet out of his teens.
The youngster wore a floppy-brimmed hat and work
clothes, and wasn't carrying a gun that Boyd could see. He
held up a hand and called, "Say, aren't you Mr. Mc-
Masters?"

Boyd brought the chestnut to a halt. "That's right, son,"
he admitted. "What can I do for you?"

"I thought I recognized you from the other day." The
young man grinned. "From that fight in saloon, you know,
when you shot off Mitch Riley's toe."

Boyd tried not to sigh. He probably would have gained
less notoriety if he had just shot that son of a bitch Riley

through the head. Folks would have forgotten about that. Somebody getting a toe blown off . . . now *that* they remembered.

"Were you looking for me?" he asked the youngster.

"Sure was. Mr. Morrison at the drugstore gave me a message to deliver to you. A telegraph, I think it is. He said to tell you he was sorry, but he was busy and couldn't find nobody to bring it out to the Fletcher place until now."

Boyd grunted. Better late than never, as the old saying went. He brought his horse closer to the youngster's mount and held out his hand. "I'll take the message," he said.

The boy nodded, and was reaching for the breast pocket of his shirt when a bullet bored through the back of his hand and slammed into his chest, lifting him right out of the saddle and knocking him onto the dirt of the road.

Sixteen

Boyd left his own saddle in a dive that sent him toward the opposite side of the road. He rolled into the shallow bar ditch there, figuring that any cover, no matter how slight, was better than none. His pistol was in his hand as he came to a stop, although he didn't remember drawing it.

The youngster's horse had bolted, and Boyd's chestnut had shied away a few steps, leaving him with a clear view of the road. The young man lay on the other side, hunched up, his uninjured hand pressed to his chest. He was moving a little, and Boyd heard him moan.

The boy was still alive. Boyd couldn't leave him lying out there in the open like that.

He glanced back along the road to the west. That was where the shot had come from, he estimated. It had to have been like that for the young man to have been struck by the bullet like he was.

Another near-miss by the bushwhacker, Boyd thought bitterly, only this time the stray bullet had hit another person, not a horse.

There were plenty of trees where the rifleman could be hiding. Boyd knew he would be risking another shot if he came out of the ditch, but he had no choice. Tensing his muscles, he sprang up and darted across the road toward the fallen youngster, jamming his gun back in the holster as he ran.

No more shots sounded. Boyd reached the wounded man, bent over, and grabbed his shirt. With a grunt of effort, Boyd rolled the youngster onto his back and dragged him toward the ditch on that side of the road. He hoped he wasn't doing any more damage than the bullet had already done.

The young man sprawled into the ditch and Boyd flopped down beside him. Drawing his gun again, Boyd lifted his head carefully. There had still been only the single shot, but he hadn't heard any hoofbeats indicating that the bushwhacker was riding off either.

Boyd looked to the east, toward Silver Creek. The settlement was no more than half a mile away, he figured, although he couldn't see it due to the trees and the hills. It was possible that someone in town had heard the shot and would come to investigate . . . but not likely. In this part of the country, one rifle shot could have any number of possible explanations, most of them fairly innocent. Chances were, he was on his own out here.

The youngster groaned again, and he said hoarsely, "What . . . what happened? I . . . I'm shot!"

"You sure as hell are, son," Boyd told him. "You'd better lie still and keep your head down. The fella who put that slug in you may still be around here somewhere."

"Didn't figure to . . . get up and . . . dance a jig."

A tight smile tugged at Boyd's mouth for a moment. The boy had sand, no doubt about that. Otherwise he wouldn't be able to make jokes at a time like this.

After a few seconds, the youngster went on. "How bad am I hit?"

Boyd looked over at the stain on his shirt. There was quite a bit of blood, but that was actually a good sign, in a way. If the bullet had hit him in the heart, there wouldn't have been nearly that much blood—plus the kid would be dead by now, of course. Likewise, Boyd didn't hear the telltale rattling wheeze which would indicate the slug had penetrated a lung. It was possible the bullet had smacked right on through, tearing up flesh, severing blood vessels, maybe even cracking bone, but still and all missing anything vital. If blood loss or shock didn't kill the youngster, he might stand a pretty good chance of pulling through.

"It's bad enough," Boyd said honestly, "but I think if we can get you into town and turn a sawbones loose on you, you'll be all right."

"We got a good doc. Dr. Steward can patch up . . . just about anything. Did my horse . . . run off?"

Boyd checked the road again. The boy's mount had only gone about fifty yards before wandering off the road and stopping to graze. The shot had spooked the animal, but it had calmed down quickly.

"I can catch him," Boyd said. "You wait right here."

"I'll . . . be here," the young man said.

He was going to have to take a chance of drawing the ambusher's fire again, Boyd knew. He stood up, holstered his gun, and strode quickly to the chestnut. The horse shied a little, but Boyd had no trouble grasping the reins and swinging up into the saddle. He rode down the trail toward the young man's horse and gathered it up as well. No one took a shot at him as he went back along the road to the spot of the ambush.

The bushwhacker must have fled again, Boyd decided, taking off for the tall and uncut when he saw that his shot had missed and hit the wrong man. Boyd's face was grim as he dismounted and knelt once more by the wounded youngster.

"Come on," Boyd said. "It'll hurt like hell, but we've got to get you in the saddle."

"I can make it," the young man said stubbornly. "Just give me a hand."

The bleeding seemed to have slowed down, Boyd thought as he helped the youngster stumble over to the second horse and grasp the saddlehorn. There was deceptive strength in Boyd's rangy, whang-leather body. He hoisted the young man into the saddle, getting some blood on his own shirt in the process.

"Hang on," Boyd said as he climbed onto the chestnut again. "It's not far to town."

The young man was leaning over the pommel of the saddle, his hands wrapped tightly around the horn. "I can make it," he said again.

Boyd caught up the reins of the other horse and started toward Silver Creek, not setting too fast a pace because he didn't want to jar the injured man too much. There was a fine line between hurrying on to the settlement to reach the doctor and not doing any more damage to the youngster. Finally, after long minutes that seemed even more drawn out to Boyd, the steeples of Silver Creek's two churches came into view, followed by the roofs of the buildings. Boyd pushed the two horses a little faster, more impatient now than ever to reach the settlement.

The sight of the youngster hunched over the saddle, the front of his shirt sodden with blood, drew a lot of attention as they reached Silver Creek. A couple of women cried out in horror, and several men ran forward to meet the two riders. "Where's the doctor's office?" Boyd demanded of them.

"Right down there," one of the townies replied, pointing to a rock house set among some trees. "I'll run tell Doc Steward you're coming!"

Boyd kept the horses moving steadily. "Almost there, son," he told the young man.

When he didn't get an answer, he looked over anxiously and saw that the youngster's eyes were closed and his face was even more pale than before. The boy had passed out, but his hands were still wrapped stubbornly around the saddlehorn.

Dr. Steward came out of his house in response to the summons from the townsman. He was a tall man, mostly bald, with heavy eyebrows and a short, salt-and-pepper beard. "That's young Dan Strayhorn," he exclaimed when he saw the wounded man. "What happened to him?"

"Rifle bullet in the chest," Boyd said curtly as he hurriedly dismounted and helped the doctor lift the youngster down from the horse. "Looks like it didn't go through, so I reckon it's still in him somewhere. Think it missed his heart and lungs, though."

Steward grunted. "He's lucky it didn't deflect off his clavicle and tumble down through his internal organs. Give me a hand here."

Working together, they got Dan Strayhorn into the house and stretched out on a table in the examining room. The doctor had other patients, but none of their needs were as pressing as the young man's. Moving quickly, Steward used a pair of scissors to cut away the blood-soaked shirt and tossed it into a corner. Then he began to closely examine the bullet wound.

Boyd stepped back. This was out of his area of expertise—if he, in fact, had one other than drinking and feeling sorry for himself. He realized he was sweating, so he took off his hat and sleeved the beads of moisture from his forehead. Then the pile of rags that had been Dan Strayhorn's shirt caught his eye.

The youngster had been reaching for that telegraph message when he was shot, Boyd recalled. He went over to the corner and reached down to pick up the bloody shirt. Grimacing and using only a couple of fingers, he was able to work a folded piece of paper out of the pocket.

The paper was flimsy to start with, and soaked with blood as it was, the words that had been penciled on it had become illegible. In fact, the paper tried to fall apart when Boyd unfolded it. He glared at the now-unreadable message in disgust for a moment, then dropped it on top of the tattered shirt.

"Ah, there it is," Dr. Steward said behind him.

Boyd turned to see the physician bent over the examining table. He had a probe inserted in the wound in Dan Strayhorn's chest, and as Boyd watched he slid a narrow pair of forceps down over the probe, following it to the bullet embedded in the flesh. When he had a firm grip on the slug, Steward withdrew the probe, then worked the forceps back out, gripping them tightly so that he didn't lose the bullet. A moment later he was dropping the misshapen hunk of lead into a basin.

"Hand me that carbolic acid," he said to Boyd, pointing with a bloody finger as he did so. Boyd brought the medicine to the table, then following Steward's instructions, opened the bottle and poured the disinfectant freely over the wound. Steward nodded in satisfaction. "That ought to keep it from festering."

"There's a bullet hole in his hand too," Boyd said.

"Already noticed that. I'll take a look at it as soon as I've got this wound bandaged."

Boyd stepped back again, and the door into the examining room opened behind him. Marshal Durkee demanded, "What in blazes happened? Somebody came and told me all hell was breakin' loose."

Boyd turned to face him and answered, "Somebody took a shot at me again. They missed and hit this youngster instead."

"Damn! That's Dan Strayhorn. I know him and his folks. Good people." Durkee glared at Boyd. "Havin' you around these parts is gettin' downright dangerous, Mc-Masters!"

"I don't like it any more than you do, Marshal," Boyd said. He turned back to the medico. "What do you think, Doc? Will the boy pull through?"

Steward hesitated, then said, "I think he will. But there are no guarantees in medicine, Mister . . . McMasters, was it?"

"That's right. Just do your best, Doctor. I've got to be moving on."

"Don't worry. I'll take good care of the lad. Someone should see about notifying his parents, however."

"I'll do that," Durkee said grimly.

Boyd strode out of the doctor's office, grateful that the

chore of telling the boy's folks he had been shot had not fallen to him. Durkee walked alongside him, and when they were outside the lawman said, "Are you plannin' on leavin' any time soon, McMasters?"

"I don't know. Why?"

"Like I said, it ain't been too healthy since you rode into town. I was hopin' you'd be ridin' out soon."

"That depends on how long it takes me to find Jonas Fletcher's bulls," Boyd said. "And speaking of that, I want to have a talk with that key-pounder over at the drugstore."

"I ain't goin' to ask why, but I'll tell you this, mister— don't start any more trouble around here. I wouldn't take kindly to it."

"I haven't started any of the trouble," Boyd snapped. "But I sure as hell intend to finish some."

He stalked off, forgetting until he had left the marshal behind that he had intended to ask Durkee about the murder of Lonnie Colson. A glance over his shoulder told Boyd that Durkee had already gone on his way, no doubt to notify Dan Strayhorn's parents of their son's injury.

Boyd went on to Morrison's Drug Store, letting the screen door slam behind him as he entered. The druggist was behind the right-hand counter this morning, instead of at the soda fountain, and he was fetching down from a shelf a bottle of tonic for an elderly female customer.

"I want to talk to you, Morrison," Boyd snapped, ignoring the glare of disapproval the old woman directed at him.

Morrison frowned worriedly. "Of course, Mr. Mc-Masters. I'll be right with you." He gave the bottle of tonic to the woman. "There you go, Mrs. Tomlinson. I'll just put that on your tab."

"Thank you, Mr. Morrison," she said stiffly. She glowered at Boyd again, sniffed, and walked out.

Morrison came around the end of the counter. "What can I do for you, Mr. McMasters?" he asked. "Did you get that telegram all right that I sent out—"

"The one you sent with Dan Strayhorn?"

"Yes, that's right. I'm sorry I didn't get it to you sooner, but it didn't come in until late yesterday afternoon, and then I had sort of a rush here at the store earlier this morning—"

Boyd was in no mood to let the man prattle on. He said, "Somebody shot the Strayhorn boy by accident while they were aiming at me. He's down at the doctor's house now."

"Shot! Dan was shot? My God!" Morrison turned pale. "Is he all right?"

"He's got a chance," Boyd said. "What I want to know now is if you've got a copy of that message you sent with him?"

"A copy?" Morrison blinked stupidly, and Boyd wondered how the man had gotten the job of telegrapher in the first place. "No, I just wrote down the message as it came in, then gave it to Dan this morning to take out to the JF Connected for you. He didn't give you the message before he was shot?"

Boyd shook his head. "No, he didn't. And he bled so much the flimsy you wrote the message on was worthless. Nobody could read it." Boyd felt his frustration growing. "You say you didn't make a copy?"

"Well, no. It's supposed to be standard procedure, but I was busy, and it was late. . . . " Morrison broke off his explanation with a sheepish grimace.

Boyd took a deep breath, swallowing the angry words that wanted to come out of his mouth. Morrison might still be able to help him. "Do you remember what it said?"

"Why, I wouldn't know. A telegram is confidential, after all."

"You had to know what was in it to write it down, damn it! Try to remember."

Morrison screwed up his face in concentration, thinking so hard that his handlebar mustache started quivering. Finally he shook his head. "Nope. Sorry, Mr. McMasters. I've trained myself over the years to forget completely about what's in the telegrams as soon as I've written them down. I just can't recollect what was in this one."

Beating the hell out of Morrison wouldn't do any good, Boyd told himself. He sighed heavily and said, "Well, if any of it comes back to you, will you let me know?"

"Sure," Morrison nodded, eager to please.

"And you've still got a copy of the wire I sent yesterday, don't you?"

"Oh, yes."

"Send it again," Boyd said heavily. "Add something on there explaining what happened. And this time when the reply comes back, get it to me right away, no matter what."

"I sure will, Mr. McMasters. You can count on me."

No, what he could really count on, Boyd thought bleakly as he pushed out of the drugstore, was a hell of a lot more trouble before he finally got to the bottom of this case.

Seventeen

He turned toward the marshal's office, but before he got there he spotted a familiar face across the street. The young woman called Rosie was walking alone there, wearing a long brown skirt and a white, low-cut blouse. Boyd crossed the street to intercept her and lifted a hand in greeting.

She summoned up a smile and said, "Oh, hello, Mr. McMasters." Her curly blond hair had been brushed, and her makeup wasn't quite as thick today. The swell of her breasts above the lacy neckline of the blouse and the painted face still advertised her as a soiled dove, but she looked fresher, less timeworn, than many such women Boyd had encountered.

"Good morning, Rosie," Boyd said, not quite sure why he had crossed the street just to talk to a prostitute. Maybe she had heard something about Colson's murder, he decided. But as shaken as she had been by the experience, he didn't want to upset her with any blunt questions. He settled instead for asking, "How are you doing today?"

Her smile weakened a little but didn't go away. "It's mighty nice of you to ask. I know you're talking about Lonnie getting killed and all. I reckon I'm all right."

"Have you heard anything about who might've . . ." Boyd let the question trail away.

"Cut his throat?" Rosie took a deep breath. "No, and I don't expect to. Marshal Durkee doesn't care about Lonnie getting killed. He's not going to waste a lot of time trying to find out what happened.''

Boyd frowned. ''Durkee's the law around here. It's his job to try to find out what happened.''

Rosie shrugged and said, ''The marshal, he just figures somebody killed Lonnie to steal his money. I think that's what happened too. I guess it'd be better if we all just sort of forgot about it. Lonnie was pretty much a no-account, after all.'' She smiled wistfully. ''But he could be really nice sometimes. I already miss him. He and Chuck used to bring me presents sometimes. . . . ''

''Wait a minute,'' Boyd said sharply. ''Who did you say?''

''Lonnie—Lonnie and Chuck. They would bring me little presents.''

''Chuck Fletcher?'' Boyd wanted to grab her by the shoulders, but he knew that doing so here on the main street of the settlement would attract more attention than he needed.

''Well, sure Chuck Fletcher,'' Rosie said. ''He and Lonnie were best friends.''

''Chuck told me he didn't really know Lonnie that well, that they just got drunk together a few times.''

Rosie frowned. ''That's just not true at all. They were always together when Chuck was in town. Well, not *always*, not when Lonnie and I were, well, you know. They weren't *that* close.''

Boyd was glad to hear it. He asked, ''Is Chuck one of your customers too?''

''Oh, no. Not that he thought he was too good or anything like that. He'd have a drink with Lonnie and me, and like I said, he brought me presents sometimes too, just little things, but he never did anything else. Lonnie told me once that Chuck was in love with somebody a long time ago, but he lost her and he's sort of steered clear of women ever since except as friends.''

The wheels inside Boyd's brain were clicking around

like those of a runaway stagecoach. He asked, "How long has it been since you saw Chuck and Lonnie together?"

Rosie didn't answer right away. Instead, she asked, "What's this all about, Mr. McMasters? You don't think Chuck could have had anything to do with Lonnie getting killed, do you? That's just not . . . Well, I can't imagine it! They were friends!"

"How long?" Boyd repeated.

"Well . . . I guess it's been about . . . three weeks, maybe?"

Three weeks. About the time, in other words, that Jonas Fletcher's four prize bulls had been stolen.

One thing didn't have to be connected with the other, Boyd reminded himself. He didn't have one damned bit of proof either way. But he couldn't help but be curious, and when he got back to the JF Connected, he intended to ask Chuck Fletcher some questions.

He intended to get answers too.

Boyd kept his eyes and ears open as he returned to the ranch, but no one took a shot at him. Before leaving Silver Creek, he had stopped back by Dr. Steward's and found that Dan Strayhorn was resting quietly. The physician was optimistic about the young man's chances for recovery.

That was at least a little bit of good news, Boyd thought as he rode. He wouldn't have wanted to be even indirectly responsible for the youngster's death.

The ranch headquarters looked almost deserted as Boyd rode up. A few men were moving around the barn and the corrals. He tied the chestnut in front of the house and went inside, his boot heels ringing on the porch as he crossed to the door.

"Anybody here?" he called. His voice echoed, making the house seem even emptier.

Sarey Beth Oliver came out of the kitchen. She greeted him with a grin and said, "Back already, Mr. McMasters? How'd it go in town?"

He didn't want to take the time to explain, so he ignored the question and asked one of his own. "Where is everybody?"

"Mrs. Sumner's lyin' down upstairs. I swear, I never saw a woman take it easy more'n that one. She's the restin'est woman I ever did see."

"What about the others?" Boyd asked, trying not to sound impatient.

"Well, Jonas promised he'd show that Miss Clark around the ranch, so they went to do that, and most of the others decided they'd go along too, which I don't think sat too well with Jonas, since I figure he thought he'd have the lady to himself for a while, but Harry and Pat ain't never happy just sittin' around when they can be up and movin', and I guess that Sumner fella was bored too—"

Boyd held up a hand to stop the flood of words from the woman's mouth. "What about Chuck—and Albie Clark?" he added as an afterthought.

"Last I saw of Chuck he was down at the barn, and I don't know where Clark is. I'm pretty sure he didn't go with the others, though. Say, he sure is an unfriendly cuss, ain't he? Always grousin' about something or other."

Boyd couldn't argue with that, but right now he was more interested in talking to Chuck Fletcher. He nodded and said, "Thanks."

"Why, you're mighty welcome, Mr. McMasters. Say, I'm bakin' an apple cinnamon pie out in the kitchen. It's Harry's favorite, and I told him I'd fix one for him while we're here. You want to come out and try a piece?"

"Maybe later," Boyd said as he turned back toward the front door.

He headed straight for the barn, hoping he could still find Chuck there. If not, maybe one of the ranch hands would know where he had gone. But luck was with Boyd for a change, and as he strode into the barn, he saw Chuck emerging from a horse stall with one of the JF Connected punchers.

"Better get a new shoe on that buckskin's left front hoof," Chuck was telling the cowboy. "I don't like the looks of the one that's there."

"Sure, Chuck," the puncher replied. "I'll take that hoss right over to the smith's and have him get started."

Chuck stopped short when he saw Boyd striding toward him. Something about Boyd's expression must have warned him, because he frowned and asked, "What is it, Boyd? Something's wrong, isn't it?"

"You could say that." Boyd waited until the cowboy had led a good-looking buckskin gelding out of the stall and started toward the big double doors at the front of the barn. Then he said in a low voice, "Somebody took a shot at me on the way into town again."

Chuck's eyes widened in what seemed to be genuine surprise. "No!" He spotted the drops of blood on Boyd's shirt and exclaimed, "You're hit—"

"That's somebody else's blood," Boyd said grimly. "It belonged to a young fella named Dan Strayhorn. He took the slug that was meant for me."

"Lord! I know the Strayhorn kid. Is he—"

"He's got a good chance of pulling through, Doc Steward says. Where have you been this morning, Chuck?"

"Right here on the ranch," Chuck answered without hesitation. "I've been checking over the riding stock, seeing which ones need some attention—hey! You make it sound like maybe you thought *I* had something to do with taking a shot at you!"

"You weren't with me either time I was bushwhacked," Boyd said coolly. "And it's not like you haven't lied to me before."

"Lied to you? Why, I never—"

"What about Lonnie Colson?"

Boyd knew from the shock and guilt on Chuck's face that his shot had found its target. Chuck stumbled, "What . . . what about Lonnie?"

"You told me that you barely knew him, that you just

got drunk together a couple of times. But now I hear that you and he were best friends, right up until about three weeks ago. Right up to just about the time those bulls were stolen from your brother.''

"Damn it, Boyd, you can't think that I . . . Why, I've been trying to help you *find* those bulls!" Chuck looked both flabbergasted and angry.

"That's what you made it look like, anyway. Maybe you were just keeping an eye on me, making sure that I didn't get too close to the truth."

"This is crazy!" Chuck practically howled. "Why would I do such a thing?"

"To get even with your brother." As he spoke, Boyd felt the pieces suddenly locking together in his brain. The vague image he had seen once before appeared again, but this time it was crystal clear. He had no proof, but he was convinced of its truth. "To pay Jonas back for driving off the woman that *you* loved more than he ever did. Belinda's *your* daughter, isn't she, Chuck? You were in love with your brother's wife."

"No!" Chuck looked stricken, all the cheerfulness that was his hallmark vanishing under the lash of Boyd's accusations. His face was pale and haggard as he shook his head. "No, Boyd, you've got it all wrong."

"Has he, Uncle Chuck?" a new voice asked from the door of the barn. "Or . . . or should I call you Daddy?"

Boyd and Chuck both turned to see Belinda standing there, and she looked every bit as shaken as Chuck. He held his hands out to her and said, "No . . . no, sweetheart, I swear to you. I'm not your father. Jonas is."

Boyd frowned. If what Chuck was saying was true, that knocked out of the props out from under one part of the theory that had formed in his brain. He said, "What about the rest of it? You were in love with Sally, weren't you?"

Chuck turned abruptly toward him, and for a second Boyd thought the man was going to take a swing at him. "Yes, damn you, I was! But nothing happened between us.

I . . . I told her how I felt, and she thought it was sweet. . . . '' A great shudder went through him. ''But that was all. To her I was just . . . a friend. Just her husband's kid brother. When she finally . . . turned to somebody else, it sure as hell wasn't me!''

''But you still blamed Jonas because she ran away, didn't you?'' Boyd wasn't ready to let go of his idea just yet. It might still hold together enough to allow him to get to the truth.

Chuck's mouth opened and closed a couple of times, and he swallowed hard. ''I thought . . . if she hadn't run off like that . . . Sally might've changed her mind about me sooner or later. She would have, I'm sure of it!''

Belinda said quietly, ''Oh, Uncle Chuck.'' Tears were running down her face as she came toward him and held out her arms. She took hold of Chuck, hugging him tightly.

He patted her back awkwardly and said in a half-whisper, ''I always tried to look after you, Belinda. You're . . . you're the picture of your mother. That's why I . . . I tried to make Jonas understand about you and Griff Torrance. I . . . I didn't want you to run away too.''

This was touching as all hell, Boyd thought, but it wasn't getting him any closer to what was most important to him. He said sharply, ''What about the bulls, Chuck? The way I see it, you had two reasons to take them: to get even with your brother for forcing the woman you loved to run off with another man, and to punish him for the way he was treating Belinda. Where are they, Chuck?''

Chuck glared at him over Belinda's shoulder. ''Damn it, Boyd—''

''Look, I know all about it, Chuck. You and Lonnie Colson stole the bulls, maybe with the help of a couple of other men. That's how come Lonnie had money for a change. You paid him off, and you avoided him for the past few weeks because you didn't want anybody getting suspicious of the two of you. The other men were just drifters, weren't they, who already moved on from Silver Creek.''

Chuck swallowed hard again and said, "I tell you, you've got it all wrong."

Boyd wasn't going to let up on the pressure. He was going to keep prodding until he got the truth out of Chuck. "You've got those bulls stashed somewhere," he went on, "and what you don't know is that you're going to make your brother lose the JF Connected. And you'll lose too, Chuck, because the ranch is half yours. Or is that another reason you've got for hating your brother—the fact that he's always acted like the ranch was his alone, instead of belonging to both of you?"

Belinda moved back a step, resting her hands on her uncle's forearms. "Is it true, Uncle Chuck?" she asked. "Did you . . . did you take those bulls?"

"I . . . I . . ." Chuck couldn't make himself speak, at least not as long as she was looking so intently at him. He pulled away from her and turned away, facing the wall with his hands clenched at his sides. In a voice that was little more than a whisper, he said, "I took them. I . . . I figured Jonas needed to be taught a lesson . . . and I thought it would be funny."

A practical joke, Boyd thought bitterly. At the heart of it, this was just another of Chuck's damned practical jokes.

"But it all went wrong!" Chuck exclaimed brokenly, turning back to them. "We took the bulls, just like you said, Boyd—Lonnie and me and a couple of men I hired. But I don't have them now, I swear it! Don't you understand? *Somebody stole them from us!*"

And with a sinking heart, Boyd knew that Chuck Fletcher was telling the truth.

Eighteen

And yet, Boyd realized a moment later, while Chuck's statement still left plenty of unanswered questions, it also made sense. Laying the blame for everything at Chuck's feet would have also meant that he was responsible for the ambush attempts, and despite Boyd's earlier question about his whereabouts, he just couldn't see Chuck Fletcher as a murderous bushwhacker.

"I think you'd better tell me the whole thing from the beginning, Chuck," Boyd said firmly.

Before anything more could be said, however, the sound of angry voices outside made all three of them turn toward the entrance of the barn. They had been so caught up in the emotional fireworks in the barn that they had not noticed the sound of horses' hooves and buggy wheels outside.

It was impossible not to notice the heated words now being exchanged, however. Boyd recognized Jonas Fletcher's voice as the rancher said loudly, "Damn it, Clark, you gave me four more days."

"Well, I made a mistake and I'm changing my mind!" Albie Clark shot back. "I want either that bull or my money back, and I want it today!"

Boyd and Chuck exchanged a glance, and Chuck began, "I swear, Boyd—"

"Save it," Boyd advised curtly. "Let's go see what this

is all about. Until we find out, we'll keep quiet about what just went on in here. You understand, Belinda?''

She tossed her long dark hair, some of the old fire back in her eyes as she replied, ''I won't say anything, not until Uncle Chuck's had a chance to explain everything.''

''And I can,'' Chuck said quickly. ''I can explain all of it . . . well, some of it, anyway.''

The three of them strode to the barn entrance to watch the confrontation going on outside. Jonas Fletcher was standing beside the buggy in which he had taken Natalie Clark on her tour of the ranch. Natalie was still seated in the vehicle, her lovely face tense as she watched her brother squaring off against Fletcher. A saddled horse was nearby, and Clark had obviously just dismounted to stand facing Fletcher, a hostile glare on his pinched features. Fletcher looked both angry and confused as he confronted Clark. Harry Oliver, Pat Sturdivant, and Enos Sumner were all still on horseback, waiting and watching near the buggy.

Fletcher was saying, ''. . . explained this over and over, Clark. You've got to give me a little time.''

''I don't have to give you a damned thing,'' Clark said. ''We had a business deal, and you didn't hold up your end of the bargain. Now I've got every right to ask for my money back, and I don't have to give you an hour, let alone four days. Any court in Texas will back me up on this, Fletcher, and you know it.''

Fletcher shook his head stubbornly. ''You said four days.''

''*You* said four days, Fletcher, not me. I may have gone along at the moment, but like I said, I've changed my mind. Now, these other fools may be willing to let you string them along—''

Enos Sumner exploded, ''Damn it, you've no right to talk about me like that, Clark!'' Sturdivant and Oliver didn't look happy about being referred to as fools either.

Clark laughed harshly. ''If you let Fletcher keep pulling the wool over your eyes, a fool is exactly what you are, all of you. Don't you see? He's been out to steal our money all along. I'm not sure there ever were any prize bulls!''

Fletcher growled a curse. "By God, you can't talk about me like that on my own land!" He reached for the rifle that was lying on the floorboard of the buggy. Clark's hand went to the stock of the Winchester that was in the saddle boot on his horse. Natalie's hands went to her mouth, muffling a scream. Sturdivant, Oliver, and Sumner let out surprised exclamations as imminent violence loomed in the air.

"Wait just a damned minute!"

Boyd's rock-hard voice cut through the tension and made Fletcher and Clark both freeze before either man could lift a weapon. Boyd strode out of the barn, followed by Chuck and Belinda. A quick glance from him warned both of them to be silent and follow his lead.

"It won't do any good for you two idiots to start shooting at each other," Boyd went on, letting his impatience come through in his voice. "That won't settle anything."

"I won't be talked to like that," Fletcher said stiffly.

"You'll take it and like it," Boyd snapped. "You got yourself into this mess, Fletcher, and now it's my job to dig you out of it." He grimaced. "It pains me to say it, but Clark's got a point. He's well within his rights to demand his money back." Boyd sent a stony look at Clark. "But that doesn't mean I'll stand by and let you two blaze away at each other."

"What *are* you going to do?" Clark demanded.

"Get those bulls back."

Clark snorted in contempt. "Today?"

"Maybe," Boyd replied levelly.

Chuck started to say something, but Boyd made a curt gesture, stopping him before any words came out. If Chuck spilled everything that had just gone on inside the barn, that would only complicate matters all the more. Boyd didn't want that right now. He wanted some time to put everything together, to try to make some sense of it all.

"I don't trust you any more than I trust Fletcher," Clark said.

Natalie spoke up, saying sharply, "Well, I do, Albie. I think you should back off and give Boyd a chance."

"Shut up, Natalie," Clark said. "This is none of your business."

"It most certainly is. I own part of our ranch too, you know, so it's my money at risk as well as yours."

Clark glanced at her, his gaze seething with anger. "I'm responsible for making the decisions."

"Well, maybe you shouldn't be." Natalie stepped down from the buggy and confronted her brother. "You don't seem to have done that well so far."

Clark trembled with anger. He looked like he wanted to strike Natalie, but he held back. Boyd was glad of that. The mood he was in, if Clark had tried to hit Natalie, he might have up and shot the son of a bitch.

"All right," Clark finally said. "You want to make the decisions, go ahead. But it's on your head now, Natalie."

"That's fine with me," she said coolly. She turned to Fletcher and went on. "I'm sorry, Jonas, but business is business. We can't give you four days to produce those bulls . . . but we can give you until tonight."

"Tonight?" Fletcher repeated. "But that's not enough time—"

"I'm sorry, I truly am. But Albie and I *do* have a great deal riding on this transaction."

Enos Sumner stepped forward. "So do I, Fletcher. You can have until tonight, but that's all."

Boyd wasn't surprised that Sumner was following the lead of the Clarks. Nor was he surprised when Fletcher sent him a desperate, questioning glance.

Boyd nodded.

"All right," Fletcher said after taking a deep breath. "If the bulls haven't been recovered by tonight, you'll get your money back—all four of you!"

"Now, Jonas," Pat Sturdivant said, "Harry and me ain't asked for that."

"It doesn't matter," Fletcher declared. "I'm going to be fair about this. It's all or nothing."

"About time," Clark said. He took his sister's arm. "Come on, Natalie."

She didn't protest as he led her toward the house. After a moment, Sumner followed them.

Sturdivant and Oliver dismounted and came over to Fletcher. "Don't you worry, Jonas," Sturdivant said. "I'm sure everything's goin' to turn out all right."

"Of course it will," Fletcher said quietly. "Of course it will." He seemed to notice his daughter for the first time. "What are you doing out here, Belinda?"

"I got tired of moping in my room," she said. "I want to help somehow."

"There's nothing you can do," Fletcher told her. He looked at Boyd. "Right now, I'd say Mr. McMasters is our only hope."

"Don't worry, Fletcher," Boyd said. He glanced at Chuck. "I'm about to get to the bottom of this. I want to get a fresh horse, then Chuck and I are riding out to follow some new leads."

"Chuck?" Fletcher sounded surprised. "Why are you taking Chuck?"

Boyd looked at the ashen-faced young man again. "Chuck's sort of my unofficial assistant," he said dryly. "I don't think I'm going to solve this case without his help."

Chuck swallowed hard and looked like a man who wasn't too happy with the confidence that had just been expressed in him.

"All right," Boyd said ten minutes later as the two of them rode away from the ranch, heading north. "Tell me about it. *All* of it. Just like you started to in the barn."

"Well, you figured out most of it," Chuck said miserably. "I was in love with Sally when I was a kid. You know how beautiful she was; you've seen Belinda."

Boyd nodded and waited for the other man to go on.

"Jonas has always sort of run roughshod over everybody in his life," Chuck continued after a moment. "I don't think he means to hurt anybody. He's just used to getting his way, and he doesn't like it whenever anybody thinks differently than he does."

"I've run across more than one cattle baron who felt that way."

Chuck nodded eagerly. "That's it. Jonas has always fancied himself to be an old-fashioned cattle baron, and he wanted folks to talk about the JF Connected in the same breath with the King Ranch or the Four Sixes or the XIT."

"Only it didn't work out that way," Boyd said. "And now he needs the money from the sale of those bulls just to keep his head above water."

"I didn't know it was that bad, I swear it," Chuck insisted. "If I had, I never would have taken the bulls—but I might have thought about it."

"You said you and Colson and two other men stole the bulls?"

"That's right. The other two fellas were just passing through, and they're long gone by now. I gave them some whiskey money and they were glad to help. But you were wrong about Lonnie. I didn't have to pay him. He helped me because he was my friend."

Boyd frowned in thought. "That girl Rosie said Colson had a whole poke full of money. Where did it come from, if not from you?"

Chuck shook his head and said, "I don't know. Like I told you, I sort of steered clear of Lonnie after we took the bulls. I thought that might be better."

"We'll come back to that," Boyd decided. "Tell me about the actual theft."

"There wasn't anything to it," Chuck said. "It was even easier than I thought it would be. We hazed the bulls north, onto that rocky ground I showed you, but we never crossed the road. We doubled back and circled around and hid the bulls in a little canyon off to the west, about as far as you could get from the ranch house and still be on JF Connected range. I can show you.''

Boyd nodded grimly. ''You'd better, I reckon.''

They turned their horses and headed west, riding for over an hour. Boyd hadn't been that far in this direction during any of his travels around the ranch, and he found that the terrain grew more rugged, just as it did to the north, across the main road on Mike Torrance's Rocking T. ''We don't use this part of the ranch much,'' Chuck explained as they rode through an area of wooded hills and brush-choked gullies. ''That's why I thought it would be safe to hide the bulls over here. I was going to make sure that any time any search parties came this way that I would be in charge of the area where the bulls really were. Jonas was so convinced that Mike Torrance was to blame, though, that he never did order a full-scale search of the ranch.'' Chuck shook his head. ''Wouldn't have mattered much if he had. Within forty-eight hours after we took the bulls from that pen, they were gone from the place we left them.''

''Could they have wandered off on their own?'' Boyd asked.

''Not a chance,'' Chuck declared emphatically. ''They were in a little box canyon, and we had a brush gate across the only way out. When I went to check on them a couple of days later, the gate was closed, but the bulls were gone. There were horse tracks around there too that hadn't been there before. Somebody opened that gate, drove the bulls out, and closed the gate behind them.''

Boyd looked intently at the other man. ''Are you sure you're telling me the truth about all this?''

''I swear to you, Boyd, I'm not hiding a thing. It's all true. I know better than to lie to you now.''

That put him almost back where he had started, Boyd thought bleakly. Almost, but not quite.

There was still a little matter of a couple of ambush attempts. . . .

The two bushwhackings might not be connected with the case that had brought him here, Boyd reflected. They could have been motivated by something as simple as a shot-off toe. He didn't really think Mitch Riley was responsible for the shots that had been taken at him, however. Boyd's instincts told him the attempts on his life were tied in with his investigation of the theft. Now that he knew Mike Torrance hadn't taken the bulls, he could also clear Torrance of the bushwhackings.

Or could he? *Somebody* had wound up with those prize bulls, and it could have just as easily been Torrance as anybody else. Another theory began to form in Boyd's brain, but he didn't have it all put together yet by the time they reached the canyon where Chuck and his confederates had brought the bulls in the first place.

"This is it," Chuck said as he drew rein in front of the isolated little canyon. It was only about a hundred yards wide and twice that deep, and it was walled by high, steep, rocky bluffs that would have been difficult, if not downright impossible, for the bulls to negotiate. The gate made out of trimmed saplings and brush was still in place. Boyd looked past it and saw that the canyon had pretty good graze on its floor, as well as a small, spring-fed pool that supplied water. It would have made a good place to stash the stolen bulls for a while, and Boyd said as much.

"I never intended for them to be there for more than a few days," Chuck said. "Just long enough for Jonas to sweat real good. Then I was going to pretend to find them and save the day. I thought that would make Jonas take me a little more seriously. He never has. Of course, most of that's my fault, because of all those jokes I've played on people. . . ."

"But when the bulls disappeared, you were afraid to tell him your part in it."

Chuck nodded. "That's right. I figured he might kill

me—or at least run me off the ranch for good. I . . . I was hoping they'd show up again, or that the law would find them. I just went on pretending I hadn't had anything to do with it. But Marshal Durkee and the sheriff weren't any help, and the Texas Rangers were too short-handed to do anything. I didn't know what was going to happen. Then you showed up.''

''And you latched on to me, hoping I'd find the bulls and your part in the whole thing wouldn't ever have to come out?''

''Yep. I'm afraid so. But I really did want to help, Boyd. I still do. I know now how much all this means to Jonas. I . . . I don't reckon he deserved so much trouble.''

Boyd wasn't sure he shared that opinion, but either way his job was still to find those bulls. He asked, ''You couldn't follow the tracks away from here?''

''There wasn't any trail that I could find. Whoever took the bulls knew what they were doing and covered up all the tracks.''

Boyd doubted that. It would have been virtually impossible to eliminate every sign of the bulls' passage. But obviously the thieves had been good enough to fool Chuck, who wasn't much of a tracker. And now, after all this time, whatever trail *was* left would be much too cold to follow.

Those ambush attempts nagged at Boyd, and so did that telegraph message from Warren he had never gotten. He still didn't see how any of the prospective buyers could have been involved in the theft of the bulls, but it suddenly occurred to him that the second attack on him hadn't taken place until Dan Strayhorn had started to fetch the telegram out of his pocket.

Could the would-be killer have been firing at the *boy* instead?

That was too far-fetched, Boyd decided, and yet maybe it had all worked out for the rifleman after all, if indeed the man's intention had been to keep Boyd from reading that message. Suddenly, whatever information had been in Warren's wire took on some added potential importance.

"Let's get back to the ranch," Boyd said abruptly. "I've got something else to do."

"You've got an idea?" Chuck asked eagerly.

"A hunch," Boyd said. "That's all."

But maybe, when you got right down to it, that would be enough.

Nineteen

All hell had broken loose by the time they got back to the JF Connected headquarters.

Belinda must have heard the hoofbeats of their horses, because she came running out of the house as Boyd and Chuck rode up. Sarey Beth Oliver followed her, and both women appeared to be quite upset.

Boyd reined in. "What happened?" he asked tersely as Belinda came up to his horse and grabbed the stirrup.

"You've got to stop him," she said. "He took some of the men and went up to the Rocking T."

"Your father?"

Belinda nodded. "He said he was going to have it out with Mike Torrance once and for all and get those bulls back."

Sarey Beth put in, "I'm afraid there's goin' to be some shootin'. Jonas wasn't in much of a mood to listen. Not after that little weasel Clark backed him into a corner the way he did."

"Damn!" Boyd had been hoping that Jonas Fletcher would continue to wait, would give him one last chance to come up with the whereabouts of those stolen bulls. Obviously, though, Fletcher's impatience, spurred on by Clark's stubborn demands, had gotten the better of him and sent him galloping for Torrance's spread, no doubt with rifle in hand. The JF Connected punchers would back him all the way too.

"Where's everybody else?" Chuck asked.

"My man Harry went with 'em," Sarey Beth answered, "along with Pat Sturdivant and that Sumner fella. Clark went too. Mrs. Sumner's inside bawlin' her eyes out. She figures her husband's goin' to get killed for sure once the shootin' starts."

"What about Natalie Clark?" Boyd wanted to know.

Sarey Beth inclined her head toward the house. "She's inside too. Told her brother that if he wanted to be a damned fool, that was up to him. She's washed her hands of the whole deal."

Belinda said anxiously, "Can't you do something, Mr. McMasters? Can't you stop them somehow before . . . before somebody gets hurt?"

Boyd knew she was talking about Griff Torrance, as well as her father. He had planned to ride back into Silver Creek one more time, in hopes that Warren would have responded to the wire that was sent earlier in the day, but it looked like there was a more pressing concern now.

"Chuck and I will ride up there," Boyd promised the young woman. "Maybe we can head off the trouble—even if it means telling your father what we found out earlier." He cast a meaningful glance at Chuck, who swallowed nervously but nodded, indicating his willingness to go along with whatever Boyd deemed necessary.

"You found out something?" Sarey Beth said. "What?"

"Sorry, there's no time—" Boyd began, but he broke off his sentence at the sound of rapidly pounding hoofbeats.

He and Chuck both wheeled their horses around to see who was coming. One man rode along the trail that led to the ranch house, and he was pushing his mount hard. As the horsebacker came closer, Boyd was surprised to recognize the druggist and telegrapher from Silver Creek. Morrison was bouncing awkwardly in the saddle. Clearly, he wasn't much of a rider, and whatever had brought him out here, it had to be important.

He was wheezing and gasping for breath as he brought his horse to a stop in front of the house. "Mister . . . Mr. McMasters," he managed to say after a moment. "I . . . I've got that telegraph message . . . for you."

Boyd remembered telling Morrison earlier in the day that he wanted to see the reply to his telegram as soon as possible after it came in. Evidently the man had taken him at his word. Morrison went on. "I got somebody to . . . watch the store for me . . . and brought this right out to you." He took a folded piece of paper from his pocket and extended it toward Boyd. The motion reminded Boyd of Dan Strayhorn's actions that morning, just before the bullet had knocked him out of the saddle.

"Thanks," Boyd said as he took the telegram from Morrison. He unfolded it and saw that it was covered with small, neat printing. Warren's reply was rather long. Boyd began scanning it quickly, his eyes picking out the pertinent bits of information. Most of it just confirmed things that he already knew about the ranchers who had come here to pick up those bulls.

But then he reached the part that read:

ALBIE CLARK NO LONGER MEMBER ASSOCI-
ATION STOP DROPPED FOR NON-PAYMENT OF
DUES STOP WACO SOURCES SAY CLARK
SOLD RANCH EARLIER THIS YEAR STOP

Boyd's fingers clenched on the paper, crumpling it slightly as the meaning of those terse sentences soaked in on his brain. Suddenly, things that hadn't made much sense before were beginning to fit together. There were two parts to the puzzle of the missing bulls. Chuck Fletcher had been one of them.

And now Boyd thought he knew the other.

He swung down from his saddle and started toward the house, the telegram clutched in his hand, prompting Chuck to call after him, "Hey, Boyd, I thought we were riding to the Rocking T to try to stop Jonas."

"There's something I've got to do first," Boyd said over his shoulder without looking back. He knew it was important to reach Torrance's ranch in time to head off any shooting, but this part of the showdown was important too.

He let the screen door slam behind him as he strode in. The sound of sobbing came from the parlor to his left. He paused in the doorway of the room and saw Annabelle Sumner curled up on a sofa, a fancy little lace handkerchief balled up in her hand as she pressed it to her eyes.

"Where's Natalie Clark?" he asked curtly.

Annabelle looked up at him in surprise. Her face was pale except around the eyes and nose, where it was red and puffy from crying. "Oh, Mr. McMasters!" she exclaimed. "You've got to stop them! Poor Enos is going to be hurt, I just know he is."

Boyd reined in the impatience he felt. If he snapped at the woman, she might just start bawling worse, which would slow him down even more. He said calmly, "I've got to talk to Natalie first, Mrs. Sumner. Do you know where she is?"

"I . . . I think she's upstairs," Annabelle managed to say. "In her room, I suppose."

Boyd nodded and headed for the stairs. He should have gone straight up and not bothered wasting any time with Mrs. Sumner, he realized. Natalie was probably packing.

His guess was right, he saw a moment later when he reached her door and kicked it open. Natalie had several valises on the bed and had obviously been busy stuffing her belongings into them. Startled by Boyd's rough entrance, she stepped back quickly from the bed and brought a hand to her breast.

"Oh, my goodness, Boyd!" she said, putting a weak smile on her face. "You frightened me. What on earth possessed you to come bursting in like that?"

"Maybe I figured if I surprised you, you'd tell me the

truth for a change,'' Boyd said coldly.

"Tell you the truth?'' Natalie repeated. "Why Boyd, I've always told you the truth!''

"Like that ranch you and your brother have down on the Brazos close to Waco?'' He raised the telegram in his left hand. "The ranch that the two of you *sold* earlier this year?''

"What . . . how . . .'' Natalie blinked in confusion. She seemed genuinely baffled.

But Boyd knew firsthand what a damned good actress she could be.

"You had to know about it, Natalie,'' he said. "You had to be in on the whole thing, right from the start. You knew you and your brother didn't have a ranch to take that bull back to. So why all the pretending?'' As he spoke, he took mental hold of the remaining pieces, shifted them around in his mind, and saw the way they fit together. A humorless smile tugged at his mouth as he went on. "You didn't have a ranch . . . but you intended to have one on the future. *This* ranch. The JF Connected.''

"I don't have the slightest idea what you're talking about,'' Natalie insisted, but instead of confusion, Boyd saw pinpricks of anger in her eyes now, anger that the scheme she and her brother had concocted had been discovered.

"One thing about civilization,'' Boyd said, "it's getting harder and harder to cover your tracks. It's not enough to hide the trail a horse or some stolen bulls leave. You've got to do something about the trail of paper too.''

"I swear, I think you've taken leave of your senses—''

"How long do you think it's going to take to find out that you and your brother bought Jonas Fletcher's note from the bank in Silver Creek? You may have slipped the banker some money to cooperate with you and foreclose on Fletcher when he couldn't pay off the note, but you don't really think the man's going to go to jail for fraud just to save your hides, do you? You might as well give it up,

Natalie. It's not going to work."

There was a step in the hallway behind him. Chuck asked, "What in blazes are you talking about, Boyd?"

Boyd's head jerked involuntarily toward Chuck. At the same instant, the hand that Natalie still had pressed to her breast slipped inside the bodice of her dress and came back out with a small pistol clutched in it. Boyd saw the flicker of movement from the corner of his eye and threw himself to the side.

The little gun cracked wickedly, and Chuck grunted. Boyd's shoulder hit the wall. He saw Natalie swinging the barrel of the pistol toward him again as he palmed out the heavy revolver holstered on his hip. He lunged forward, lashing out with the weapon.

The barrel of the gun caught Natalie across the wrist. There was a snapping sound, and she let out a scream as her pistol slipped from her fingers and thudded to the floor. She staggered back, clutching her broken wrist with her good hand.

Boyd kicked the little pistol well out of reach with the side of his foot, then glanced over his shoulder. Chuck was leaning against the wall on the far side of the hall, blood staining the left shoulder of his cowhide vest. He was staring at the blood that was also on his right hand, which he had been using to grip the wounded shoulder. He looked up at Boyd and said in amazement, "I've been shot."

"That's the third time a bullet meant for me has hit the wrong target," Boyd said, "and the second time Natalie fired it."

"You bastard!" she grated at him. "You broke my wrist!"

"You killed a good horse when you bushwhacked me the first time," Boyd snapped back at her.

"That's insane! I . . . I was with that cowboy—"

"On the way into town maybe. What did you do, tell him you could handle the buggy yourself and send him back early? That'll be easy to check too."

"I . . . I wanted to be alone. He had his saddle horse tied to the back of the buggy, so I told him he could go back. But that doesn't mean I shot at you!"

"Everybody else was together, except for your brother, and he was busy with something else. You were the only one unaccounted for that time—except for Annabelle Sumner, and I don't reckon she's the bushwhacking type."

Chuck said, "I'm still bleeding out here, you know."

Before Boyd could say anything, Belinda and Sarey Beth came rushing along the hall in response to the shot. Belinda cried out, "Uncle Chuck! You're hurt!"

While the two of them tended to Chuck, Boyd looked at Natalie and went on. "Both of you had to be working together. You took the shot at me yesterday, and your brother tried to ambush me this morning when a youngster from Silver Creek got shot by accident. But it worked out for you, at least for the time being, because that boy was bringing me a telegram with the same information as this one. I wasn't able to read it, though, since it was soaked in Dan Strayhorn's blood. That gave you and your brother time to back Fletcher into a corner and provoke a shooting war with Torrance. You were probably hoping Fletcher would be killed so that you'd just have to deal with Chuck when it came time to take over the ranch."

"Hey," Chuck said weakly from the hallway, "I think I resent that."

Boyd ignored him. "I don't know how you found out about Fletcher's money problems. I reckon you've been on the lookout for a setup like this for a while. Or maybe your brother just decided to buy that bull, looked into Fletcher's situation as a matter of curiosity, and realized how he could wind up owning the whole place, not just a bull." Boyd glanced over his shoulder at Chuck. "Whose idea was it to steal those bulls for a joke, Chuck? Was it yours—or was it Lonnie Colson's?"

Chuck blinked owlishly. "Well . . . I think maybe Lonnie first brought it up, after I'd been drinking with him and grousing about Jonas, but . . . that would mean Lonnie was working with that Clark fella all along!''

Boyd nodded and said, ''That's how it looks to me.''

''Damn! And I thought Lonnie and me were friends! He must've shown Clark where we hid the bulls.''

Sarey Beth Oliver said, ''I'm as confused as a calf that's lost its mama. Chuck, you mean to say *you* stole those bulls?''

''It's a long story,'' Chuck said sheepishly. ''And I'm *still* bleeding.''

''Come on downstairs,'' Belinda said. ''We'll get that wound tied up, then put you in a wagon and take you to town so Dr. Steward can take a look at it. I don't think it's very bad, though. Looks like a pretty shallow crease to me.''

''Oh, yeah, a shallow crease,'' Chuck complained as the women started to lead him away. ''It's not your shoulder that feels like it got kicked by a mule.''

Belinda looked back over her shoulder at Boyd.

''There's still the problem of my father. He and the other men are probably at the Rocking T by now.''

''I know,'' Boyd said grimly. ''Mrs. Oliver, why don't you let Belinda help her uncle? I need you to keep an eye on Miss Clark here.''

''I reckon I heard enough to know she needs some watchin' over, all right,'' Sarey Beth replied. ''I'll fetch my greener.''

''You can take her to the doctor too. She'll need that wrist set and splinted. Then see if Marshal Durkee's got room for her in his jail.''

Sarey Beth nodded emphatically and followed Belinda and Chuck. Boyd had waited this long; he could wait long enough for her to return with her shotgun to stand guard over Natalie.

''Boyd . . .'' Natalie said, her voice revealing the pain of her broken wrist and the desperation she had to be feeling. ''I . . . I just can't believe you'd do this to me. Not after what we had together.''

"You mean the way you came to my bed so you could keep an eye on me and find out just how much I'd figured out?'' There was a bitter taste on the back of Boyd's tongue. "You must've been damned happy to discover I was still in the dark.''

"You . . . you could have come in on it with us. I could have talked Albie into going along with it.''

Boyd's eyes narrowed as he looked at her. Even pale and shaken and defeated, she was still undeniably beautiful. But there was nothing inside, nothing to compare to what he had found first with Hannah, then with Martha Blair in Oklahoma City. He had been a fool, all right.

But it wasn't like this was the first time. . . .

"Sure," he said with a dry chuckle. "I could have gone in on it with you, just like Lonnie Colson did. And one of these days I'd have wound up with my throat cut, just like Lonnie. That's what your brother was busy doing while you were deciding to ambush me. He doesn't like to leave anybody behind who might talk, does he?''

She must have seen that she wasn't going to get through to him, because she sighed and said, "Boyd . . .it wasn't all acting when I was with you. It really wasn't.''

"Maybe not," he told her, "but it doesn't matter. It doesn't matter a damn.''

Twenty

Somehow it had gotten to be late afternoon, Boyd realized as he rode hard toward the Rocking T. The day had been a full one, and he recalled that he hadn't eaten since breakfast that morning. He had covered a lot of ground—and uncovered a lot of villainy—since then. But he wasn't hungry. The things he had discovered along the way had pretty much taken care of his appetite for the time being. Betrayal and deception had a way of leaving a bad taste in a man's mouth.

By now one of the ranch wagons from the JF Connected would be on its way to Silver Creek, taking Chuck Fletcher and Natalie Clark to the doctor. After that, Natalie would be going to jail. Maybe she'd only killed that grulla horse, but it hadn't been from lack of trying. Besides, she had to have known about her brother's murder of Lonnie Colson, and that knowledge made her an accessory. She'd spend some time behind bars for her part in the scheme.

Boyd couldn't bring himself to feel sorry for her.

He crossed the road to Silver Creek, and started up the trail to the Rocking T. Jonas Fletcher and his men had been gone for quite a while, and Boyd knew he wouldn't reach the Torrance spread in time to head them off. But maybe nobody had started shooting yet. . . .

That hope was dashed a few minutes later when he heard

the distant crackle of rifle fire floating through the hot Texas air.

"Damn!" Boyd grated as he leaned forward over his mount's neck and urged more speed out of the horse. If he had gone through everything only to be too late . . . if more men had died because of Albie Clark's plotting and scheming . . . then he would settle this with Clark, once and for all, and the legalities be damned!

The shots grew louder and more frequent as Boyd approached the headquarters of the Rocking T. Some of the landmarks were familiar from his visit the day before. As he sent his horse up a long hill, he realized that just over the crest of the rise was the valley where Torrance's ranch house was located.

Another volley of shots rang out as Boyd topped the hill. Immediately, he saw that his fears were in the process of coming true. The JF Connected men were ranged through the trees on the hillside, using the trunks for cover as they poured rifle fire at the dogtrot cabin where the Torrance forces were holed up. Powder smoke hung in a haze around the cabin as the men inside returned the fire through broken-out windows and rifle slits. Boyd caught a glimpse of someone lying sprawled motionless in the dogtrot. A curse hissed between his teeth.

He hauled his horse to a stop and swung down rapidly from the saddle. A stray bullet could easily reach up here to the top of the hill. Moving quickly, he led the horse into a thick growth of trees and wrapped the reins around some brush. Several other horses bearing the JF Connected brand were tied there too, out of harm's way. Boyd pulled the heavy .70-caliber rifle from its sheath and hurried to the edge of the trees, where he dropped to one knee to study the situation.

If he could get Jonas Fletcher's attention, he might persuade Fletcher to call off the attack. But the Torrances and the other men in the cabin couldn't hear him, and they would keep shooting. Somehow, Boyd had to deal with them first.

One of the pecan trees behind the cabin was close enough so that the branches overhung the roof. It was difficult to judge at this distance, but Boyd thought some of the branches were directly over the stone chimney. Smoke curled from that chimney, indicating that there was a fire in the fireplace. The men inside wouldn't need it for heat on a day like today, but there was a good chance they were boiling water to cleanse bullet wounds. Boyd didn't care about the reason; he just hoped he would be able to make the shots he wanted to make. He lifted the rifle to his shoulder and drew a bead on one of the branches above the cabin.

The rifle boomed, and he saw the branch leap as the heavy slug struck it. The branch sagged but didn't break off. Boyd aimed carefully and fired again, and this time the bullet clipped through the part of the branch that was still attached to the tree. The branch dropped straight down to land on the chimney.

Boyd lifted his sights and fired again. The roar of the rifle had slightly deafened him, so he couldn't hear the shouts from the JF Connected men as they swiveled their heads and looked up the slope to see who the newcomer was who was taking a hand in the fight. He saw their reaction from the corner of his eye, however.

His third shot was a clean hit, separating another branch from the tree. It fell atop the chimney with the other one, and the thick foliage blocked the opening to a certain extent. Some smoke still filtered through between the leaves, of course, but enough of it backed up to be making it pretty unbearable inside the cabin. Boyd wondered how long it would take before the Torrance forces were driven out.

In the meantime, he heard Jonas Fletcher shouting, "Hold your fire! Hold your fire!"

Fletcher was still alive, Boyd thought. That was good.

He didn't want Albie Clark winning even the slightest victory.

He stood up and watched the cabin as the gunfire died away. Smoke billowed from the windows, and it seemed impossible for anyone to stay in there much longer.

Boyd's gaze darted around, seeking Clark. After a moment he found the man, standing behind some oaks with Harry Oliver, Pat Sturdivant, and Enos Sumner. From the looks of it, none of them had participated in the battle between the JF Connected and the Rocking T. Fletcher wasn't far away, looking back up the slope at Boyd in surprise and anger. Boyd started down toward Fletcher, bending over to make himself a smaller target just in case any more shots came from the ranch house.

"It's about time you got here," Fletcher snapped. "We need all the guns we can get to deal with those thieves. Of course," he admitted grudgingly, "that was a pretty good idea you had, blocking the chimney with those branches like that."

"You'd better just hope not too many men are dead down there," Body said, his voice every bit as hard and angry as Fletcher's. "If they are, they died for nothing."

"What the hell are you talking about? I know Torrance stole those bulls. He's finally getting what's coming to him!"

Boyd thought for a second about slapping the stock of his rifle alongside Fletcher's head to see if that would knock some sense into the man. Instead, he said quietly, "Torrance didn't steal your bulls. I know that now."

Fletcher's eyes widened. "You found them?"

Before Boyd could answer, one of the JF Connected punchers yelled, "They're comin' out!"

Sure enough, the door of the cabin had burst open, and several men stumbled out, coughing and hacking from the smoke that filled the building. But they hadn't given up the fight. They had pistols in their hands, and they opened fire on the hillside as they fled the cabin.

"Hold your fire!" Boyd bellowed to the JF Connected punchers, hoping they would obey him. To Fletcher, he said, "Tell them not to shoot!"

Fletcher hesitated as the guns from the Rocking T men continued popping. Then he added his shout to Boyd's. "Don't shoot, boys! Hold your fire!"

Boyd recognized Mike Torrance down below, followed by his son Griff. Lifting the rifle to his shoulder again, Boyd took aim and put a slug in the dirt at Torrance's feet. The bullet kicked up dust into eyes that must have already been stinging and watering from the smoke. Torrance stumbled forward a couple of more steps, then stopped and looked around in confusion.

"Drop your guns, Torrance!" Boyd shouted, his voice carrying clearly. "It's all over!"

Griff Torrance swung toward Boyd and lifted his six-gun, but before he could squeeze the trigger his father grabbed his wrist and forced his arm down. "Hold on!" Torrance cried. "No more shootin'! We're puttin' our guns down!"

He and the half-dozen or so men with him did as he ordered, although Griff dropped his gun only reluctantly. They stumbled forward, wiping their eyes, as Fletcher's men emerged from the cover of the trees and covered them cautiously.

Fletcher looked at Boyd and said gruffly, "Thanks for your help, McMasters. We can handle it from here. Torrance will tell me where those bulls are, or so help me, I'll string up him and every one of his men, including that son of his!"

Boyd's hand shot out and gripped Fletcher's arm as the rancher started to turn away. "Damn it, don't you ever *listen?* Torrance didn't steal those bulls! He's innocent, you stubborn son of a bitch!"

For a second, Fletcher obviously thought about lifting his gun and taking a shot at Boyd, but the cold look in the CPA agent's eyes—and the fact that Boyd was still holding that big rifle—made Fletcher pause. He said, "If Torrance didn't take the bulls . . . then who did?"

"Your brother," Boyd said flatly.

"Chuck? Hell, you're crazy!" Fletcher stared at Boyd in astonishment.

"Chuck took them," Boyd went on, "but he doesn't have them now. Somebody else stole them from Chuck."

"Who?" Fletcher demanded.

Boyd turned to face the four men who stood nearby. "Albie Clark."

Clark's eyes widened in surprise and hatred. "That's a damned lie!" he exploded. "Why in blazes would *I* steal those bulls? I wanted to buy one of them!"

"What you wanted," Boyd said, "was to take over the JF Connected. You wanted those prize bulls—*and* Fletcher's ranch."

Fletcher was shaking his head. "I don't understand any of this."

"Neither did I until a little while ago," Boyd admitted. "Then it all came together when I got this telegram from my brother." He took the crumpled piece of paper from his shirt pocket and thrust it at Fletcher. At the same time, he kept an eye on Albie Clark, not trusting the man who had already proven to be both devious and ruthless.

While Jonas Fletcher was reading the telegram, some of the JF Connected men brought Mike Torrance and Griff up the hill at gunpoint. The rancher and his son both had hate etched in their faces. "Fletcher!" Torrance shouted, then turned the air blue around his head with a string of curses.

"Nobody was killed, Boss, just shot up a little," one of the punchers reported to Fletcher, raising his voice to be heard over Torrance's profanity. "That fella we downed in the dogtrot was creased pretty good, but some of the boys are patchin' him up right now. I reckon he'll be all right."

"You ride in here," Torrance sputtered, "call me a thief, start shootin' without any warnin' . . . I'll . . . you damned . . ."

"That's enough," Boyd said loudly into the confusion. "Everybody settle down."

Albie Clark pointed a shaking finger at him. "You accused *me* of being a thief, McMasters! I won't stand for that. I'll have you fired! I'll haul you into court! I'll—"

"You'll shut up," Boyd told him, shifting the barrel of the rifle to cover the livid Clark.

Fletcher looked up from the telegram in his hands. "This says Clark doesn't even have a ranch anymore. Why did he want one of those bulls?"

"Like I tried to get through your thick skull a minute ago, he wanted *your* ranch, Fletcher. He was going to get it by buying your note from the bank, then making sure you couldn't pay it off. He figured out you needed the money from the sale of those bulls to pay off what you owed. So he tricked Chuck into stealing the bulls from you. Then he stole the bulls from Chuck, or had them stolen. I imagine he's got them stashed somewhere, so that once he had control of the JF Connected, he could bring them back and sell them off himself or even keep them and improve the herd that much more."

Fletcher was still frowning in confusion. "It's damned hard to believe."

"That's because it's a lie!" Clark howled.

"Your sister is probably behind bars by now, Clark," Boyd said. "You don't really think she's going to take the blame for everything when she can lay most of it off on you, do you?"

"Miss Natalie was part of it too?" Fletcher asked in amazement.

Boyd ignored the question. He saw the realization sinking in on Clark. The man knew now that his plan had failed. Sturdivant, Oliver, and Enos Sumner began edging away from him, looks of contempt on their faces. Probably none of them fully grasped all the implications of Clark's scheme, but they were all range men.

They knew a sidewinder when they saw one.

"You son of a bitch," Fletcher breathed as he glared at Clark. "You nearly ruined me. And you nearly made a murderer out of me too. I was ready to kill Torrance and all of his men for something they didn't do."

Torrance said, "Damned well about time you figured that out, you hotheaded son of a bitch!"

Fletcher turned to face him. "I . . . I'm sorry, Torrance," he said with a heavy sigh. "I never knew—"

"You never stopped to think!"

Boyd cut in. "You two can mend your fences later, if you want to bad enough. Right now there's still Clark to deal with. I imagine there's room in that cell with his sister. He'll swing for murdering Lonnie Colson. That's what he was doing when he pretended his horse was lame and slipped off from that sight-seeing tour of your ranch, Fletcher."

Fletcher turned to face Clark again and abruptly started toward him. "That's for the law to hash out," Fletcher said angrily. "I want my damned bulls back! Where are they, Clark?"

"Wait a minute, Fletcher!" Boyd called anxiously, taken by surprise by the rancher's sudden move.

But it was too late. Fletcher had put himself between Clark and the others, and the man was going to take the desperate chance Fate had offered him. Boyd saw the flicker of motion as Clark yanked a gun from a cross-draw rig under his coat.

"Get back, goddamn it!" Clark cried. He lunged for a horse tied nearby as he pulled the trigger and the pistol cracked.

The bullet hit Jonas Fletcher and drove him backward as the other men around him scattered, diving for cover. All except Boyd McMasters, who brought the rifle to his shoulder and fired as Clark tried to leap into the saddle. The heavy bullet with the carpet tack shoved into its nose caught Clark in the side and spun him like a top. He slammed to the ground, already more dead than alive, but somehow he managed to not only hang on to his gun but even lift it again. Boyd saw the muzzle of it trying to come into line with him as he levered another .70-caliber round into the chamber and pressed the trigger again.

This bullet slammed through Clark's chest, pulping his heart and pinning him to the ground, arms outflung. He never got his second shot off.

Boyd strode over to him to make sure he was dead, even though there was little doubt in his mind. As he peered down at Clark, he felt mixed emotions. He couldn't bring himself to be sorry that the man was dead, but at the same time it might have been more fitting if he had met his end on a hangman's gallows.

Well, either way, Boyd decided, dead was dead, and Albie Clark would never scheme again.

"The bastard shot me!" Jonas Fletcher said behind Boyd, sounding amazed.

"And you deserved it," Mike Torrance said.

Boyd couldn't argue with that. Fletcher had nearly plunged this part of the country into a bloody, useless range war, just because of his irrational dislike of the Torrances. Boyd turned and saw that Clark's shot had clipped Fletcher on the hip, creating a bloody but not too serious wound. With the rifle in his hand hanging at his side, Boyd walked over to where Fletcher was sitting on the ground.

"You're a lucky man, Fletcher," he said. "You're going to get those bulls back once we find out from Natalie where they are, you probably won't lose your ranch, and you didn't kill a bunch of men for nothing. Maybe if you're really lucky, your daughter and your brother will forgive you for being a horse's ass all these years, and you'll see that Mike Torrance here could be a good friend to you— if you'll let him."

Torrance stared. "Me, friends with this . . . this—"

"Better than being enemies," Boyd said.

Then he turned, walked back to his horse, and slid the rifle into the saddle boot. Fletcher and Torrance could work things out if they wanted to; that was none of his business. As soon as he located those bulls so that they could be returned to Fletcher, his job here would be done.

He jerked the reins loose from the brush, swung up into the saddle, and rode away.

Twenty-one

Chuck found Boyd in the barn the next day, saddling the horse Jonas Fletcher had given him for the ride back to Oklahoma City. Chuck's shoulder was bandaged and his left arm was in a sling, but he didn't seem to be in much pain as he came up to Boyd.

"Getting ready to ride, eh?"

Boyd nodded. "That's what it looks like, isn't it?"

"Well, yeah. I was just hoping you might stay around here a little longer. You know, make sure that everything works out all right."

"It's not my job to see that everything works out all right," Boyd told him without looking at him. As he drew the cinch tight, he went on. "I was sent down here to find out what happened to those bulls and get them back if I could."

"They're not back yet," Chuck pointed out.

"They will be."

Before she found out that her brother was dead, Natalie Clark had confessed to Marshal Durkee and a Ranger captain who had been called in from the post at Veal Station. It had all been Albie's idea, according to Natalie, which came as no surprise to anybody. He had discovered Jonas Fletcher's precarious financial situation after agreeing to buy one of the bulls, and had realized how he might manipulate things so that he would wind up controlling the JF

Connected. He had traveled to Silver Creek several times before what was supposed to be his first visit, scouting out the terrain and learning about Chuck Fletcher, who had wound up being used by Clark to start the ball rolling. Natalie had also admitted that the bulls were hidden on a farm near Mineral Wells that her brother had rented under a false name. Some of the JF Connected punchers had already started over there, accompanied by the Ranger captain, to retrieve the bulls, and they would be back in a day or two. Boyd felt justified in calling his work done and starting back to Oklahoma City.

Leading the horse by the reins, he walked toward the door of the barn. Chuck hurried along beside him.

"Listen, Boyd," Chuck said eagerly, "why don't I go with you?"

That made Boyd stop and frown at the other man. "What in the world for?"

"Well . . . I could be your partner. I told you I wanted to be a range detective, and I . . . I sort of helped you solve this case, didn't I?"

"Chuck," Boyd said slowly, "there wouldn't have *been* a case if you hadn't taken those bulls in the first place."

Chuck grimaced. "Yeah, I know. And now that Jonas knows all about it, even though he's not pressing any charges, I reckon he's going to be pretty slow to forgive me. Especially since I had to tell him why, and about how I felt about Sally and all. I think it might be better if I got off the ranch for a while and did something else. You know, sort of got out from under Jonas's shadow."

To Boyd's way of thinking, Chuck should have done that a long time ago—but that didn't mean he was ready to take on a partner. He said, "Don't you think it might be better if you stayed around here to help out Belinda? She's got some things to work out with your brother too, and I reckon she could use an uncle on her side."

"Well, you're probably right. But Belinda's going to be fine now that she and Griff Torrance are getting together.

Jonas and Griff's daddy aren't going to have any choice but to get along. They're going to be related!''

Boyd led the horse outside, Chuck still following him. Boyd said, "I'll talk to my brother about you when I get back to the office, Chuck, but I can't promise anything. I don't know if there are any openings for field agents right now."

"I could work with you unofficial-like," Chuck offered.

Boyd shook his head. "I pretty much work alone. That's the way I like it. Besides, I'm really not very good company a lot of the time. You could ask a lady in Oklahoma City about *that*."

Chuck looked crestfallen. He sighed and said, "Well, if you say so, Boyd. But if you ever get back this way . . ."

"I'll be sure to stop by and say hello," Boyd said.

That brought a grin to Chuck's face again. He held out a hand as Boyd swung up into the saddle, and Boyd leaned down to shake hands with him. "You keep an eye on things around here," Boyd told him. "I reckon you're about as sensible as anybody in these parts."

"I am?" Chuck said, looking amazed. "Nobody's ever said that about me before!"

Boyd grinned back at him, turned the horse, and heeled it into a trot. He glanced back to see Chuck waving at him, a big smile on the man's face. "Don't forget to tell your brother about me!" Chuck called.

Boyd waved, then turned his attention to the trail. He'd tell Warren all about Chuck Fletcher, all right. But he wouldn't wait until he got back to Oklahoma City to do it. He would stop on his way through Silver Creek and pay another visit to Morrison's Drug Store so that he could send a wire to Warren concerning Chuck. But it wouldn't necessarily be a recommendation.

It was going to be a warning.

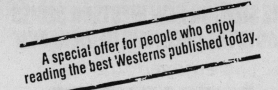

A special offer for people who enjoy reading the best Westerns published today.

WESTERNS!

NO OBLIGATION

Mail the coupon below

To start your subscription and receive 2 FREE WESTERNS, fill out the coupon below and mail it today. We'll send your first shipment which includes 2 FREE BOOKS as soon as we receive it.